BAUHINIA JUNCTION

MILLS & BOON LIMITED
LONDON · TORONTO

First published 1971

© Margaret Way 1971

Australian copyright 1979
Philippine copyright 1979

Reprinted 1979

ISBN 0 263 73136 7

Set in Linotype Plantin

Made and printed in Great Britain by
C. Nicholls & Company Ltd
The Philips Park Press, Manchester

CHAPTER 1

LIGHTNING forked through the piled-up rain clouds. There was a crack of thunder and the rain came down; no miserable dirzzle, but soaking, pelting rain. It burst from the sky in an ancient fury, cascading in waterfalls off sloping awnings and richocheting off the wet roads and pavements. Gena loved it; the spectacle of mighty nature; those flashes of elemental power that lifted a day above others. She felt it, enjoyed it with an intensity no words could express, though sometimes she thought of it as an emotional kinship with nature.

The sky looked wonderful, like one of the great moments of creation or an awesome El Greco of black and charcoal with dazzling shafts of revealed splendour – a stark backdrop for the soaring city buildings. She stood for a moment, lost, in a rain-shrouded world with the scent like no other fresh in her nostrils; the incomparable scent of rain.

The amber light flashed at the intersection, then the green. Gena roused herself and dashed madly along with everyone else to shelter at the other side. It was more than usually hazardous, she thought wryly as she dodged the glittering jewel flashes of emerald, and ruby and amethyst – the spoked flowers in the rain. Cars and buses and taxi-cabs nosed in relentlessly, waiting for the pedestrians, notoriously careless of life, to clear the swollen crossings.

There was another terrific clap of thunder and everyone ducked instinctively. Gena looked up at the storm, seeing only what seemed to her, fabulous splendour. Ever since childhood, a storm had been a significant experience for her reducing to minimal all the little faults and follies of her day. Lightning seared across the city with the magic of a master, lending it an unearthly clarity. There was nothing quite like those momentary illuminated vistas, Gena reflected half hypnotically. Spectacular as it was, this particular thunderstorm had been predicted by the Weather Bureau for late afternoon, yet very few people thought to bring in any form of protection.

Gena, at least, had a newspaper. She deposited it sodden and unread in a litter-bin, reflecting that she was far from being the only one with such a makeshift idea. It was, in fact, a well ingrained habit with most of the population not to be caught dead carrying an umbrella, for this was Brisbane, capital of tropical Queensland, the tourist's paradise with possibly the finest climate in the world. In the crowded streets there was that charming intimacy that came with lowering skies and the shared excitement of the frantic dash for cover. People chattered and laughed and indulged in a battery of watery complaints under the complex arches of boutiques and department stores.

But if they were truthful they would have admitted that they rather enjoyed it, for even the charms of Paradise benefited from a little variety!

Gena sheltered beneath a mauve and gold awning, shaking her head like a thoroughbred filly. Raindrops scattered and she flicked at the hem of her leaf-coloured skirt, damp but mercifully shrink-proof. She

6

looked up absently only to encounter the brilliant dark gaze of an Italian migrant, his skin swarthy against the impeccable white of his shirt. The admiration in those sultry eyes was so explicit that few women could have borne it without self-consciousness. Gena flushed and hurried on, young and lithe-limbed.

By the time she reached the bus stop the storm was all over and the re-entry of a brilliant sun made the past scene a memory that shimmered off the steaming pavements. Her chunky green sandals were damp, the shoulders of her slinky filamel print and the tips of her long blonde hair. But her precious drawings were safe . . . and dry; neatly tucked away in her portfolio. Gena was a commercial artist and a very recent collaborator with a well-known writer of children's stories. Her illustrations, at once charming and original, had a freshness and verve that earned her the job. The latest batch of sketches were to complete the saga of *Koko the Bush Koala in the Never-Never Land*.

A piercing, two-noted whistle issued from a blue Mustang hardback. It brought her sufficiently out of her abstraction to assume an expresion of hauteur. Despite her hauteur the Mustang swiftly reversed and pulled into the kerb beside her. Gena was ready. She had already thought out a dozen different rebuffs.

"Hop in, gorgeous!" The voice was young, masculine, and very confident. She lowered her head to encounter a brown satyr head, snapping brown eyes, ringed by what could only have been, on a girl, false eyelashes. Relief flooded her, and her eyes showed a hundred dancing lights.

"My mother told me . . ." she began lightly. The well-dieted matron beside her edged in closer just to remind her.

"Hop in, doll. This *is* the bus stop! " the confident voice cut her off laconically.

"Right! " Gena argued no longer. The bus was coming and she had quite an audience in the queue. Some for, some against, depending on the age group. Inside the car the atmosphere fairly crackled.

"Now what did your mother tell you, dear?"

Her luminous eyes slid over the slick young profile. "If you can't lick 'em, join 'em! "

White teeth flashed in his brown face. "I'm looking forward to meeting your mother."

Gena smiled. "Can't be done, Tony. Mamma is wary of types like you."

"The long-haired bizarrie?" he inquired satirically.

"Long arms, Grandma."

Tony had the grace to colour, remembering their last meeting, but his sideways glance was unabashedly admiring. Tony's world was full of pretty girls, but Gena, he concluded, was different. Totally herself. Aware, confident, a little challenging, emancipated as they all claimed to be, but for all that, deeply feminine. She excited and intrigued him, and that for Tony was an irresistible combination. If pressed he would have said he was something of a connoisseur of young women, and Gena was one to judge others by.

She turned to gaze back at him with her cool, rain-coloured eyes. They were doe's eyes, darkly fringed, and they imparted a ravishing, quite unexpected piquancy to

8

an otherwise classical face.

"Well?" Her hair slid forward like polished silk and it cost him an effort not to put out a hand to it.

"I was just thinking what a delectable dish you are, Gena. Some girls are all brains and no sex appeal or all sex appeal and dismally dim, but you've got style and character. That indefinable something a rising young reprobate needs if he's going to amount to anything in the abominable rat race." His flickering smile was cynical. "Quite frankly, pet, I don't think I'll make it on my own. I need the love of a good woman. Failing that, I haven't got that up and at 'em approach like my illustrious dad."

Gena looked at him reflectively. "Well, you are a vaguely improbable barrister. How did you come to it in the first place?"

Tony's long mouth quirked, not humorously. "Can you see the son of Ian Carson, Q.C., in anything else? Dare I be ..." he suddenly changed vocal style ... "the unthinkable thing ... a racing car driver?" Tony had a gift for reproducing voices and the cold cutting tones were undoubtedly his father's.

Gena's eyelashes lay in dark fringes against her cheeks. She sensed the old, unspoken defeats, but only murmured lightly, consolingly, "If you want the feminine angle, I'd say you were a darn sight better off. What odds thrills versus an early demise?"

Tony turned his head, the look in his impudent dark eyes almost a kiss. "None when I look at you. There's something about a long-limbed blonde ... I don't know exactly what it is, but it has enchanting results." Gena

9

grimaced and he changed the subject neatly, sensing her impatience with compliments. "What do you think of the road rocket, angel? Impressed?"

"Very."

"Enough to have dinner with me tonight? Boy scout behaviour, I promise." His eyes, had Gena been looking, gave her the lie.

She let the moments slip by just to tantalise him. "Let me think about it, Tony. Ooh, lovely!" She sank back into the plush upholstery. "The vehicle must have been terribly expensive."

Tony grinned, pleased with himself. "Give me the luxuries of life, angel. I can dispense with the necessities."

"Is that original?"

"If it's not, let it pass." Tony took his eyes off the road and smiled at her. Something flickered between them. Adroitly Gena steered the conversation into chosen channels. She was very adept at the give and take of social chatter. They began to talk of other things ... the pleasantly meaningless gossip of their set.

They had known one another only a few short weeks, but theirs had been an instinctive chemistry. Gena liked Tony, but she was slightly wary of him. In many ways Tony Carson was a very spoilt young man with the spoilt young man's idea that girls were like rosy summer apples to fall at a touch. Not so Gena. She had a very clear picture of the woman she wanted to be; unshakably at the top of the tree.

The Mustang cruised through the city's heart and the downtown streets of summer bustling. Young couples with arms entwined jaywalked through four lanes of converging traffic while a policeman stood in the centre of all this, imperturbable, blessing his new summer uniform, at long last, with *short* sleeves. They joined the endless two-way procession of traffic that streamed over the smooth sweep of steel that spanned the river, then swept on out to the suburbs.

Children tumbled and played noisy games on their own green front lawns surrounded by the exotic flora of summer. Theirs was a blessedly free existence, for the cult of one's own quarter of an acre was a recognised symbol of Australian suburbia. The Mustang drifted through corners and turned down the quiet beautiful avenue where Gena lived. Only the magnificent shade trees were long established, for the houses were dashingly modern. Tony pulled into the entrance to the pebbled drive and they watched the lazy descent of the lavender blue bells of the jacaranda as they fell on to the bonnet of the car. The air was delicious after the rain and heady with the fragrance of the countless frangipani that starred every garden.

Tony looked up at the house, his eyes narrowing appraisingly.

'*Chez* Landon! Very nice too. Cool perfection like you, doll. Your father's the best!" He opened the door for her, his long arm across her body hard and firm and vibrant. "Well?" Her mouth tilted with mischief and his glance steadied on its full lovely curves. "What's it to be, Gena girl? Are you twelve or twenty? Decide!"

Long lashes veiled the doe's eyes. "About seven o'clock," she said crisply, not giving herself a chance to

11

turn back. "Do come in and meet Mother."

"Nothing on God's earth would stop me!" Tony took his arm away, deadly serious. In his eyes was the unmistakable expression of a young man intent on the chase. Gena swung her long legs out of the car. The wind touched her dress and stroked her hair. She put up a restraining hand and the fabric of her dress tightened around high breasts and narrow waist. Tony's eyes lit appreciatively; a masculine and very natural reaction to her feminine posture, so charmingly and unconsciously provocative.

"Don't get too serious, Tony," she warned him. "It's absolutely fatal!" Her eyes widened and slanted down at him, glimmering with the eternal allure of Eve.

"Try and stop me!" He switched on the ignition, one part of him applauding the high-performance revs of the engine. He looked up at her with careful dark eyes. "I'll be on my best behaviour with Mother. I'm taking no chances with a girl as distracting as you, Gena."

Her limpid eyes were impish with laughter. "I consider you a very dangerous young man, Tony."

"You're very wise!" Tony smiled at her, small creases in his cheeks. "*Au 'voir, ma belle!*"

Gena stood watching until the Mustang disappeared, then she turned and walked up the drive with her sliding, graceful walk. The orchid-like flowers of the Cape chestnut were beginning to unfurl and she stopped to admire them, looking up at the house. It spelt beauty and peace and security; set in its large garden of native trees and shrubs. It was built to her father's design; contemporary, two-storey of western red cedar and clinker brick. Louvred doors opened out on to a cool, deeply shaded veranda and the glassed-in rear of the house extended out on to a large informal entertainment area with a pool and a tennis court. Gena's father, a whipcord forty-seven, was something of a physical fitness fanatic and she gave a small indulgent smile at the thought of his exorbitant pride in clearing the tennis net.

Inside the house, Linda was poised on the oiled maple stairway busily examining a big, heart-shaped leaf of the flamingo flower. It was only one of the many lush-leafed indoor plants from her beloved bush house. She looked up and smiled her vaguely heart-breaking smile.

"Hello, chick! I don't think this is getting enough moisture. I'd better stand it in a bowl of water." She tipped a loving finger to the waxy orange blooms.

Gena laughed, a clear, high, youthful laugh. "The theatre has lost a great actress! You were at the window peaking. Don't think I didn't notice the curtains moving." She hadn't, in fact, but played along with her usual hunch where Linda was concerned.

Her stepmother gave a slightly shamefaced grin as she walked down the stairs, a small, slender brunette in her late thirties. She looked nowhere near it with her short dark curls and Delft blue eyes. To Gena and her father, who loved her, Linda had an odd, entrancing charm.

"Never trust the glamour boys in super-charged sports cars," she said earnestly. "They could exhibit the same characteristics."

Gena's short explosive laughter cut her off. "Well, you'll have a chance to find out. Tonight! He's dying to meet you. We're going out for dinner."

13

Linda looked slightly apprehensive. "Ho, ho, so that's the way the wind blows!"

"Not at all!" Gena curled her long, lovely, colt-like limbs up on a swivel chair with beautiful precision, and regarded her stepmother with affection. "There's no need to go into an anxiety state just because this particular young man is not matrimony bound. We're just good friends. Repeat: Just good friends!"

For three long years now, Linda's well-intentioned meddling in Gena's affairs of the heart had bordered on the absurd.

Linda put out a hand helplessly and laughed. "I can't seem to help myself — another odd habit that's grown on me. I've been anxious about you ever since I took you on years ago, when a leggy ten-year-old was showing every sign of developing into a luscious young thing. I still look at you with a touch of wonder." She gave her sweet candid smile, her mind going back over the years. It was quite true Linda took her responsibilities as stepmamma very seriously indeed, aided and abetted in the early stages, at least, by Gena and her father. There had always been a silent conspiracy between them to make Linda feel needed. Her nature demanded it and both father and daughter willingly sacrificed a little of their own enviable self-sufficiency. In return Linda lavished her love on them with touching gratitude . . . shy, selfless Linda with her ready affection.

Among their own circle it was regarded as one of the great contradictions of human nature that Paul Landon, a brilliant and successful architect, had chosen as his second wife pretty, gentle and *so* retiring Linda Ross. His

14

first ecstatic young love, Virginia, had not survived the birth of her daughter. The shock and the frozen misery of it had kept him inviolate all through Gena's young childhood, but then nature had reasserted itself.

Linda had been his secretary, petite, pretty, reliable and as unobtrusive as an office fitting. When her mother, her only relative, was killed in a car smash it had been Paul Landon who had broken the news to her, and the feel of her slight, sobbing, utterly defenceless body had gone straight to his heart. This was the first stirring of total involvement and a late-flowering love. Within eighteen months they were married – some said as a mute protest against the charming, forceful ladies of Paul Landon's acquaintance.

But whatever the reason, the marriage was a success. Paul Landon was the great miracle of Linda's life and he proved a devoted and forbearing husband. As Gena grew older between the two of them, they solved all the problems of the family, for Linda, as she was the first to admit, was socially inadequate. She tried and she tried, but it remained a fact. The security of a happy marriage had improved her, but only slightly. She was a very fluttery hostess, haunted by visions of failure – a drawback, one would have thought, for a man whose business demanded the fostering of social contacts. Something of that nature must have been occurring to her then, for she looked at Gena with her great helpless eyes.

"By the way, darling, you won't go out Saturday evening, will you? Your father wants to have a few people in to dinner."

Gena looked at her with sharp compassionate eyes.

"No, of course not. Not if you need me." She bit on her lip, her mind already on a thousand practical matters. "How does oyster bisque strike you, followed by duckling in red wine with new potatoes, green peas, little carrots and perhaps a tossed salad — and that gingered apple crumble of yours is divine."

Linda smiled, greatly heartened. The kitchen was her domain, where she came into her own. She was an excellent and surprisingly an adventurous cook, but serving the food up to strangers, much less talking to them, absolutely petrified her. Gena could manage all that. It just came naturally. She could mix with any age group, find all the right words. Despite her very real affection for her stepdaughter, Linda still did not understand her. Their natures were so different, but she would have given a great deal to possess Gena's beauty, élan and vivacity, not so much for her own sake as for her beloved Paul's.

"Perhaps you could ask your young man?" she ventured.

"Perhaps," Gena agreed absentmindedly. "Something I'm by no means certain of. He would have to work out all right tonight. By the way, his name is Tony Carson, son of the illustrious Ian Carson, Q.C., though you might not believe it when you see him." She shot up abruptly from the chair and stretched her rounded golden arms.

"Now what shall I wear? Everything in my wardrobe is out! out! out!"

"Goodness, it was in! in! in! a week ago," Linda replied quite seriously. "What about the slinky new thing? It's lovely. Shows off your figure."

"Shows off your figure?" Gena turned on her. "What

16

a contradiction you are, Lindy!"

"I suppose I am!" Linda regarded her with ingenuous surprise. "I can't help thinking a girl as beautiful as you should be quickly and safely married to a fine upstanding man like your father." Her eyes momentarily glowed with love. "I'm interested to see how this young man shapes up. I shall be fiercely Mamma, I warn you."

"You couldn't be fiercely anything, poppet," Gena walked past her and patted her arm, "that's why we love you."

CHAPTER II

BUT Linda *was* fiercely Mamma, or as close to it as she could possibly get, dividing Gena and her father between amusement and chagrin. It was quite clear to both of them, but mercifully not to Tony, that Linda had taken one of her rare dislikes to someone.

It was a relief to be out of the house, Gena decided, though her father, with his easy professional charm, had saved the situation from sheer domestic farce. At least he had decided to reserve his judgement of the young man, the oblique inquiries regarding present position, bank balance, prospects, until a more suitable date, should that date ever arise. *Ian* Carson was well known to him through Rotary dinners. Gena couldn't go too far wrong there, he argued, providing it followed – like father, like son!

Of course it didn't, but no one was to know that. Tony, was on his super-best behaviour. He was young, charming, intelligent, and spoke with the slightly formal deference of a young man of his particularly fortunate background. Linda wasn't deceived! She sincerely believed a man showed his character in his choice of a car.

It wasn't until they were sipping their second aperitif that Gena found herself relaxing. The glassed-in eyrie of the Top of the Town was the current "in" place and it did offer a sweeping, full-circle panorama of the city. To Gena the twinkling, myriad coloured lights of the metropolis were far less dazzling than the night sky of the tropics with its blazing, dancing, outsize stars. Only the soft, muted music, the chatter and low recurrent waves of laughter stamped the scene with reality.

"Fruit of my heart!" Tony murmured soulfully, leaning across the table towards her, his eyes very black. In the soft pinky-gold flare from the table lamp Gena looked exquisitely fragile, animated yet dreamy, in her clinging silvery dress, but her voice was very modern with a certain amused edge to it.

"Said like a true Muslim, Tony. The only catch being, a woman is supposed to keep her mouth firmly shut."

"Not *always*, dear," Tony pointed out dryly, his eyes on her own full, curvy offender. "It seems quite remarkable that I've been able to snatch you from the bosom of the family. Stepmamma seems over-protective. I fear she took me for an inveterate wolf with her little white lamb unguarded."

Gena stiffened, forever on the defensive where Linda was concerned. "You don't *really* look wicked, Tony, though you try very hard. Linda's very sweet and very dear to me. She's the complete reversal of the fabled stepmother."

"And to think you never told me!"

"What?" She opened wide her luminous grey eyes.

"The stepmamma bit, as if you didn't know." Tony rushed in where angels feared to tread. "They seem an odd pair. One would have thought your father would have married a handsome, outgoing creature like himself."

"He did *once*," Gena pointed out crisply. Her mother had been considered one of the prettiest girls of her day and Gena had reason to be grateful for the powers of heredity. Tony, had he realised it, was beginning to prick the bubble of contentment. Any implied criticism of Linda always set her seething. What was it about Linda that called forth these comments? It seemed she'd been listening to them all her life.

"All the stranger, then," Tony persisted unwisely. "Of course it's only *my* opinion, dear."

"And *your* opinion, *dear,* is not complicated by any knowledge of the subject. I'd rather we dropped it."

"Ouch!" Tony covered his face with his hand. "Remind me not to open my mouth. You're a shining example to the females of my acquaintance, pet. They never fear to sink the boot. There's really only one thing you lack."

"What's that?"

"A man!" Tony smiled at her with unshakable equanimity, covering her hand with his own. "But you're in my clutches now." He leered at her and paused hopefully.

Gena laughed in spite of herself. "You've got winning ways."

"I think I have. Though I really thought I'd have to beg for a glance there. Family loyalty is always very touching if a somewhat unknown quality to me."

The waiter was hovering attentively and Tony began to order with considerable aplomb: Avocado and oyster cocktail for two, followed by Lobster Creole for Gena and a fillet of beef with wine sauce for himself. Naturally this set them bickering amiably over the choice of wine. A red with lobster was unthinkable, equally a white with beef was out of the question. Finally two bottles were called for: a Hunter red for Tony and a Great Western dry white for Gena's lobster.

She studied the low centrepiece of creamy tropical orchids, shot with crimson and gold. "A full bottle to myself. To make me talk, I suppose?"

"To make you more receptive." Tony endeavoured to look villainous and succeeded quite well. "Come on now, Gena, say you find me more attractive than you care to admit." He looked into the depths of his wineglass, twirling it idly.

She held him in her contemplative gaze. "Narcissuslike, he seeks to find his own reflection." A smile glimmered at the back of her eyes.

Tony absentmindedly caressed the dark hair that curled into the nape of his neck.

"Do you think I'm not sincere?" He lifted his dark eyes to her.

"Illogical, I know, but there it is." A half smile teased her mouth. Tony looked away from it with an effort.

"I can see I'll have to work harder!"

Over a superb dinner he continued to do just that, and Gena was young enough to be impressed with the way the evening was going. Tony, she found, could exhibit a very pretty wit and her low, rather exciting gurgle of laughter was all the encouragement he needed. He raised his wineglass to her, enjoying a flash of inspiration:

"If to her share some female errors fall,
 Look on her face and forget 'em all!"

Gena smiled appreciatively. "With a little practice, Tony, you'll make the perfect admirer."

Laughter leapt into his eyes. "That's what I thought myself."

The waiter appeared to sweep away the dishes from

the main course and the flaming strawberries were prepared at table. For a few moments Gena forgot Tony as she concentrated on the technique to hand on to Linda. The waiter, conscious of such an appreciative audience, wheeled and turned with the grace of a matador. The sugar and butter was caramelised in a shallow pan over low heat, then simmered with orange juice and Grand Marnier. The strawberries were added and finally cognac poured over and the whole dish ignited. It was quite a simple process, but it looked and tasted marvellous with the strawberries and sauce spooned over luscious scoops of ice-cream.

Gena and Tony spooned into it with the simple, uncomplicated pleasure of the young. Minutes later, without warning, Gena's heart began to hammer. She lifted her head in surprise, alerted to almost anything.

It was the voice she heard first; a deep, resonant voice with a faint suggestion of arrogance and the complete self-assurance of the very wealthy. There was a momentary hush of collective focused attention and Gena found herself staring . . . along with everyone else; something she would never normally have done.

The woman was strikingly elegant in a tiger lily print revolving around a lavishly female figure. She had flaming red hair, a very white skin and glistening dark eyes. She may have been slightly past her first youth, but she was unquestionably very fetching to the eye. A sophisticated blasé woman of the world.

The man was a match for any woman. Gena studied him surreptitiously from under her eyelashes. Tall, powerfully built, an inch or so over six feet, he had a very definite teak tan face, the cheekbones a fraction too high, the mouth clearly defined over a squarish deeply cleft chin. His was the look of a swashbuckling hero, intensified by the irreverent set of his arrogant dark head. He was, in fact, the living reincarnation of every dashing, larger-than-life-size character Gena had ever read about.

She shivered – a feline frisson of antagonism, like a kitten stroked up the wrong way. But it was his walk more than anything else that held every last woman in thrall, for he moved with the easy, rippling articulation of an uninhibited creature of the wild; as alien in that confined, over-civilised setting as the sudden appearance of a mountain cat. He turned his heavy dark head with its crisp dark curls and Gena caught the sheen of his eyes. She had never seen such eyes. Strange, burnished, tawny as a cougar's, the irises flecked with fire burnt in by a tropical sun, they radiated pride and a fiery kind of masculinity, a high-handed mastery that set her teeth on edge. She sat there snared in her observations, her young piquant face remote and preoccupied.

The woman put a hand to her companion's arm, spoke a word to him, and he gave her a slow careless smile, white and challenging. "Predictable!" Gena thought dispassionately, understanding the woman's quick sparkling look. She didn't care for a man so devastatingly male, she told herself. Such a man brought out all that was wilful and capricious in her. Apparently feeling her stare, the man turned. For a moment the tawny eyes held her own and Gena eased out a long fluttery breath. The eyes flickered, as though in recognition – that undecided "do I or don't I know you" look. Gena returned the look calmly from under her delicate arching brows. She had never seen anyone remotely like him in all her life, yet he continued to gaze at her thoughtfully. The most curious sensation was beginning to assail her and her head took off and floated in the air like spun glass. It must be all that glorious wine, she explained it away to herself. Gratefully she looked towards Tony, her link with reality.

"There goes a man whose demands are fulfilled much too quickly!"

To her surprise she spoke in a completely level voice.

"Nothing wrong with her either!" Tony hissed succinctly. "Passion's plaything, no less. Actually I know *him*, or rather know of him. Cyrus Brandt. He was in the office this very day. A client of Dad's. He handles all his affairs. You're looking at one of our all-powered cattle barons and no meagre matrimonial prize. He's fabulously wealthy, I believe – owns that big property out in Western Queensland, Bauhinia Junction. Along with all his other interests, mining, I think. The stud specialises in Brahmans or Santa Gertrudis, that sort of thing." Tony shrugged delicately, fastidiously, very vague about livestock.

Gena tore her eyes away from the silken flow of muscle. The cattle baron was wearing a beautiful tropical silk suit with the sheen of bronze. The tailoring didn't fall far short of perfection. "He's not very characteristic of a cattle man," she said wonderingly.

"He's not very characteristic of *anything*," Tony amended. "Now *she* looks like she's got quite a past. And that neckline! One step short of a suicide leap!" His dark eyes glittered. "I'd say she's schemed and intrigued all

24

her life . . . but with skill!"

"Gosh, you're horrid!" Gena laughed, seeing out of the corner of her eye waiters converging on a secluded table.

"Nothing less than the best for Mr. Brandt," Tony observed dryly. "Even Dad drops his 'Damn your eyes' manner with him."

Gena suddenly thought of something that was teasing her mind.

"You know, I have an old uncle, a great-uncle, actually, who lives out West. My mother's side of the family. He would know our Mr. Brandt, I feel sure. My mother spent a lot of her childhood in the Outback on Uncle Raff's property. We haven't heard from him in years. The connection was broken when my mother died. He must be quite an old man now." She smiled with sudden impishness. "I do believe I'll start up a correspondence."

"Why the big interest in Cyrus Brandt?" Tony asked point-blank.

Gena opened her eyes wide in astonishment. "Did I say anything about Cyrus Brandt? I thought we were talking about my uncle."

"You lie in the most poetic fashion, darling. But little girls and bad liars should stick to the truth." Tony's mobile mouth moved cynically and he signalled to the waiter for coffee and liqueurs. Tony had an obstinate streak in his nature and he didn't mean for Gena to get away from him. So far as he was concerned, Gena was going to some lengths to hide her interest in Mr. Cyrus Brandt, on whom, Tony was forced to admit, Fortune had poured out far too many gifts.

25

He looked across at her. Her head was tilted to one side, drooping on its long graceful neck. Her downbent face looked mysterious, enchanting, slightly moody, her mouth curving with unconscious longings.

"I feel as if I've been marking time until I met you." Tony burst out. The words just presented themselves. He had no prior intention of saying them.

She looked up to smile at him and the demure look was completely dispelled.

"Why have I suddenly become the girl of your dreams?"

"The bottle of wine, I suppose," Tony shrugged with mock derision. There was no sense in trying the rushing technique, he told himself. It worked with nine out of ten of the chicks, but instinct told him it was the wrong approach with Gena. A too heavy touch on the reins and she would be off and away from him with a toss of that long blonde mane of hers! He was determined to bide his time until he felt more secure. Gena's delicious coolness was only a façade, he was sure of it! Her mouth was undeniably ardent, as enticing as a pomegranate.

Couples began to circle the small dance floor with dreamy abstracted expressions and Gena and Tony joined them. The second time round Tony caught the cattle baron's eye and they exchanged a silent acknowledgement. Of course he would have spotted me in the office, Tony thought, rather flattered. Those strange eyes would never miss a thing. Gena, at least, wasn't aware of him, though Tony registered with a pang that this wasn't at all mutual. The cattle baron's burnished eyes were studying Gena in detail – impassively, Tony judged, but quite thoroughly. There was nothing covert in the glance. It was the frank absorbed stare of a collector face to face with an antique. Still, it was better than the questing, hungry looks Tony had intercepted more than once that evening. Gena had the sort of looks that invariably turned men's heads. It was no surprise at all when Cyrus Brandt stopped by their table, later on in the evening. Tony had been expecting it. He rose at once. His position in his father's office was soon clarified and introductions made.

Gena maintained her air of mystery with an effort. The only real strength a woman has, she thought, trying to look enigmatic. Keep up that air of mystery even if it kills you! Her hand clenched under the table, her nails biting into her palm with the strain of it.

"I know you, surely, Miss Landon?" the cattle baron was asking without preamble. His was an actor's voice, Gena decided; deep, beautiful, conscious of its own power.

"I think not," she answered mildly enough.

"I beg your pardon. Forgive me." The powerful shoulders bowed with ironic respect, while Cyrus Brandt transferred his attention to Tony. "I rang your home several times earlier this evening, but alas! no answer. I had an appointment with your father for eleven o'clock tomorrow morning, but unfortunately I've since had word that I'm needed back at Bauhinia. Would you convey my apologies to your father? I'll be flying out at first light. Unavoidable, I'm afraid, and I do dislike leaving impersonal phone messages."

"Why, certainly, I'd be glad to." Even the normally

poised Tony was stammering faintly, under the spell of the man's magnetism.

Cyrus Brandt turned briefly to Gena, a faint smile hovering about his shapely mouth. "Forgive my unforgivable crime, Miss Landon."

"All is forgiven, Mr. Brandt," she returned sweetly.

An ironic light glowed in his eyes. He lingered a moment longer, powerful, elegant, satirical.

"Perhaps destiny may cross our paths again," he drawled, his eyes on her face and gleaming shoulders. A shocking emotion seized her.

"I live in hope." She spoke in her sweetest tones, staggered by her quick upsurge of temper. A natural devil possessed this man, but there was an answering white fire in her. She looked no higher than the deeply cleft chin in the dark amused face, recognising for the first time the ancient state of war between man and woman.

He laughed softly with a flicker of cruelty. "It's always gratifying to score a triumph, Miss Landon. However, I'll take my leave of you before you think of something really inexcusable." He bowed again with elaborate taunting grace and was gone.

Tony looked hypnotised. " 'Strewth! I guess Lucifer would look like that."

"He looks more like a gentleman adventurer to me," Gena volunteered swiftly, unexpectedly catty. She took a fierce little sip of wine.

"But what a presence!" Tony's earnestness ran away with him. He didn't even hear her. "The mind boggles at his approach, though. Haven't I seen you somewhere before! I thought that line went out with plus-fours. I'd never have thought it of a man with his magnificent pan-ache." One eyebrow shot up as he studied the unwonted colour that surged beneath the smooth perfection of Gena's skin.

"You'd hardly expect too much finesse from a cattle-man," she countered illogically. "The head-on approach must have worked for years."

"Well, it's certainly worked with our flame-haired beauty! She's looking pretty mesmerized at the moment. Not popular with her own kind, I imagine. But with the men . . . delectably corrupt!"

Gena cut through the tomfoolery. "That I can well be-lieve, but she's a damn sight too old for him!" Even to her own ears her voice sounded incredibly waspish and she could have bitten her tongue out. Something that had stirred her miraculously was now having the most per-verse effect on her.

Tony sat bolt upright, half amused, half surprised. "Let's try to be fair, pet. It would be a dull old world if every lady minded her virtue. She looks perfectly delight-ful to me. All in all a mouthful. Thirty is far from over the hill, you know." Tony looked judicious. "Ripe fruit is very tempting to the connoisseur."

Gena, deciding to lapse into a discreet silence, burst out laughing. "How exquisitely apt! I know who's cor-rupt, Tony. It's you." If Tony's estimate of the red-head's age fell a good seven or eight years short of her own there was no need to mention it. Strange, she thought, she wasn't normally catty, but then she had never been tested!

From that moment on the evening seemed to flag for

her. Gena paid lip service to the conversation, trying with all her might to revive her flagging interest in Tony. Tony, for his part, continued to watch her with subdued anticipation.

In the car park they witnessed Cyrus Brandt like a great, powerful cat, putting the redhead into an automobile with a price tag all its own. Gena turned away with a flicker of pure dismay. Tony came up short.

"God, when did they let that out of its cage!"

"It looks more like shameful self-indulgence to me," Gena commented, now set on her course of strong disapproval.

Tony turned to look at her pityingly. "A car is a lovesome thing, Gena, not a wicked extravagance. That's what you females don't seem to appreciate. Besides, little possessions of that nature wouldn't make any impression on Mr. Brandt's bank balance."

The object of his appreciation slid past them noiselessly. Tony almost gagged on his breath. "Did you see it? Poetry in motion. An Alfa Romeo Veloce. And that console! A jolly old Boeing pilot would feel at home behind it." His eyebrows came together thoughtfully. "Had a funny tinkle in the rear shockers, though, didn't you think?"

Gena laughed. "Forget the snaky bit, Tony. You know darn well you'd give your eye teeth for it."

He turned to smile at her. "Full uppers and lowers, dear. It's a wonder they let us in with such distinguished company. Ah well, let's get the sporting bomb out of here."

On the way home, of course, Tony forgot all his good

intentions. The bottle of wine and two Tia Marias had gone to his head and he automatically concluded that he was entitled to the full run of the road.

Gena watched his Grand Prix manoeuvres in clearly defined traffic lanes with a monumental calm. His accompanying conversation suggested amorous scuffles to come which she was in no mood for. Clear of the city, Tony suddenly flung the car into a hairpin bend, commenting unnecessarily that he was geared too high for it.

"I don't know about you, Tony," Gena bit out when she straightened, "but I, for one, don't propose to die like a Roman candle."

"Nonsense, pet! Your nerves just need strengthening." Tony looked over at her and winked. "You did say you were in a hurry."

"Not to be killed. If you must rush the scenery, try not to do it sideways."

Tony chortled, not in the least abashed. "That's right below the belt, love, and well you know it. Now what say we go for a glorious burst down the bay? Throw caution to the winds! A moon over the waters . . . a balmy sea breeze in our faces . . . me . . . what more could you want?"

"What more indeed!" Gena murmured, wondering if perhaps she was a bad drinker. She felt surprisingly sober and contemplative.

Tony glanced in his rear vision. "I'll swear there's been a car following us. Is there?"

"Not unless it's a harp quartet," Gena drawled without turning.

Tony began to react to her change of mood.

31

"Goodness, I'm getting quite another picture of you, pet. You've rather a sharp tongue, haven't you, old girl? Just sit back and relax. I'm a very good driver."

"But I'm a very poor passenger. Pull over, Tony. I'm getting out, before we have a patrol car beside us." Tony did pull over to the side of the road.

"You're putting me on, little lady. You've just got to be. Do you know how many dolls would like to take your place? Besides, the night's but a pup!" He was pleading now, noting with alarm the intelligence and determination not even her extravagantly feminine eyes and mouth could cover. She seemed completely mistress of the situation.

"Drat all you females!" Tony burst out a shade vindictively. "You just don't understand the pull of a big V-8 engine."

But something very powerful was pulling at Gena. She opened the car door herself, feeling she had no control over what her body chose to do.

"There's a cab stand over there, Tony. I think I'll just trundle home at a sedate thirty-five."

Tony was nearly crying. "I've never heard anything so damned stupid in my whole blameless life! It's that Brandt fellow who's upset you. You were all right up until then. He's a wildly unnerving sort of bloke, even I can see that. You're simply not yourself!"

"But *you* are!" Gena countered swiftly, now determined not to proceed a foot further with him. There was more than a scrap of truth in what he was saying and the knowledge made her resentful and uneasy. "Good night, Tony," she said in a kinder voice. "No hard feelings. I did enjoy the evening up till this point. You're terribly attractive, you know, but just that teeny bit immature."

"What do you want, for God's sake!" Tony burst out, cut to the quick. "A knight in shining armour, along with his limited horsepower?" His dark eyes glittered maliciously. "You know, Gena, I think you suffer from a father fixation!"

"And I hope I don't see your funny face for a hundred years!"

Tony looked askance. He gave a short brittle bark. "You can skip the courtesies, doll."

"You can't win 'em all!" Gena retorted, as coolly possessed as when she had begun. She closed the door on him with extreme deliberation and left without another word. Tony was breathing heavily. He really shouldn't have said that bit about her father. She was really very well adjusted, if given to perversity. Nasty of her to say that about his funny face. He watched helplessly as she walked to the well-lit cab stand. There were four cabs waiting. There would be no difficulty there. What a strong-minded female! Tony found himself wishing she wasn't quite so beautiful. He roared off in a fierce agony of rejection.

Gena didn't turn her head but crossed the road swiftly. She felt vaguely disillusioned and unhappy. She wasn't really being ridiculous, she told herself. There was an important distinction between being careful and being ridiculous. Tony had been driving much too fast. In the soft, sultry air a sleek streamlined vehicle slid past her and stopped just ahead. Gena knew who it was even before the driver unwound his long length and moved towards her with that matchless grace. She had known all along that this would happen. But convention demanded she go through the preliminaries.

"What are you doing here?" she asked in a tense, husky voice.

"Waiting for you." His voice floated mockingly on the night air, knowing all the questions, all the answers. "Children really shouldn't indulge in adult vices, Miss Landon. I had a feeling you'd need rescuing before the night was out."

Her pale head tilted imperiously. The moon shone full on her face. "I beg your pardon," she said with icy dignity, now completely taken over by her mood of strangeness and presentiment.

Even in the night his eyes gleamed like a cat's. "So, an icy, calculating beauty from a sweet, ill-mannered brat. Tell me, do you melt like snow at a touch?"

Her body was as taut as an arrow ready to fly from the bow. "I really don't know what you're talking about. Tony ... Mr. Carson ... usually does *exactly* what I want."

He laughed. "You're very fortunate, then. I would have thought you'd be all things to one man and a positive threat to the rest."

Gena shivered in the warm tropical night, taking stock of his height, his powerful shoulders, his superabundant vitality.

"No, Miss Landon," he jeered softly, "you haven't fallen out of the frying pan into the fire. Impudent young schoolgirls aren't in my line."

"So I've noticed!" she returned very smartly. His hand

34

shot out and closed around her wrist, and the world suddenly took on new colours!

"Relax, child, you're like a kitten pulling on its ribbon!" Gena bit hard on her lip, angered by the sudden intimation of the ecstasy this man could arouse in a woman. How utterly senseless to feel an ache of desire!

"But I don't know you," she muttered fiercely, not realising that her nature craved the rich and vivid and vital, for she was all those things herself.

His voice was indulgent. "Ask me some questions and I'll try to answer them. Failing that, I may be able to produce some credentials. Would a driving licence and a pilot's licence do?"

She made a soft helpless exclamation and he seemed to relent his mocking attitude.

"Come now, little one, allow me to take you home. *Safely* this time. I did happen to notice your young friend's enthusiastic run of the road. Quite apart from that, he should be horsewhipped for leaving you at this time of night."

She tried to divine the expression on his face, but the moon was behind him. Anxiety lay darkly on her.

"I told you," she tried to exonerate herself. "Tony usually does what I tell him."

"How absurd!" He compelled her towards his car, so very much taller than her that she had to tilt her head to speak to him.

"This is not really necessary, Mr. Brandt, and I'm rather unhappy about it. I fully intended to take a cab."

He clicked his tongue. "You know, little one, I think you find it agreeable to be disagreeable."

35

He bent to unlock the car and she moved swiftly away from his restraining hand. It shot out and recaptured her.

"Quick thinking, but not quick enough. I really won't eat you!" From the sound of his voice he was most definitely laughing.

She bent her pale head, showing him very meek eyelids. "I think you must have me stereotyped a dumb blonde?"

He put her into the car before answering. "But aren't you acting true to type?"

Her eyes flashed fire on ice, but he only laughed. Obviously *his* evening had gone well for him, but where was the wicked lady? Gena restrained an overwhelming impulse to ask him, knowing full well he would ignore such childish impertinence.

She watched him walk round to the driver's seat, easing his long length into the seat, that had been custom built for him. His strange eyes gleamed at her.

"Don't fight it, Miss Landon. The worst is over. I'll deliver you safely home to Poppa. You look a daddy's girl."

"What an extraordinary assumption!" she managed to get out, mindful of Tony's parting shot. A daddy's girl! What on earth was he talking about?

The cattle baron shrugged rather elegantly. "You were born to be some man's treasured possession. I'd say from the look of you Daddy hasn't yet relinquished the title."

She turned towards him in a fine rage, with all a young girl's horror of appearing an inexperienced ninny.

"Are you trying to tell me I'm just a green girl?"

"Exactly," his very white teeth flashed. "But don't worry about it, little one, time will take care of it."

"As long as *you* don't take care of it!" she burst out unthinkingly, then subsided against the back of the bucket seat, leaving him a sure victory.

"Didn't I say my taste didn't run to doe-eyed school-girls a little too fond of backchat? But five years from now . . . who knows?"

"I don't feel we'll have anything in common . . . even then!" she flung the words at him, then looked out the window, feeling the whip of the wind on her hot cheeks.

He slanted a glance at her, an amused twist to his voice. "I never take any notice of what women *say*. Now, young lady, you'd better give me some directions. You might not have noticed, but we're cruising around in circles at the moment. Though I must say I'm enjoying it."

Gena sat up straight and proceeded to give him very detailed instructions indeed.

He held up a long-fingered hand. "Don't add fuel to the fire! I'm fairly well acquainted with the city. Now, may I be permitted to ask your Christian name . . . without suffering a setback, I mean."

"Gena – Genevieve," she said swiftly.

"It suits you!" The light from the dash showed his ruggedly masculine profile. It held something far stronger than mere male beauty. It was at once strange and disturbingly familiar. His physical radiance was a terrifying thing, filling the automobile with a live presence. Gena had to forcibly remind herself that they had only just met. He seemed so very much the complete person, vivid and vital with every outward sign of success. A kind of panic was growing in her, an extra-sensitive awareness of his closeness.

37

She asked her next utterly amazing question: "You're not married, Mr. Brandt?"

His brief laugh held very real amusement. "From the sound of your voice, that's a plain refusal to think otherwise."

She permitted her gaze to wander in simulated idleness over his face. "Well, you do have an unbridled look about you."

He regarded her fleetingly through half closed lids, though there was nothing sleepy about his gaze. "Perhaps I agree with the wise man about marriage ... a young man not yet; an older man not at all."

Her musical voice fell almost flat. "I find a man's natural aversion to marriage very touching."

"That does sound cynical, Miss Bristle Brush! Why, I'd be the first to admit a woman has a magical way of transforming the environment ... a curve of the cheek, a turn of the wrist ... rain-coloured eyes." His eyes flickered over her, dancing with life. "Occasionally I even find myself responding to the siren song ... the alluring inconsequential magic ... much against my better judgement!"

She tilted her head. There was a spark of amused malice in his voice, that she just could not stand! It would be a positive pleasure to slap him down.

Her voice was like honey, sweet and insinuating. "Such condescension, Mr. Brandt! It doesn't surprise me in the least that you find woman one of nature's more agreeable blunders."

His glance touched her classic profile, the shadow that rippled across her face.

"Said with just the right mixture of bravado and recklessness, though there's food for consideration there." Even the attitude of his body was amused and indulgent as though it would take far more than a schoolgirl thrust to pierce his supreme self-confidence. "You know, Gena," he turned to smile at her, "there's the same easy magic in handling women as horses. Just show 'em who's master!"

Gena's eyes sparkled and he bit off a laugh. "Oh, really!" she said, half smiling. "But predictable, Mr. Brandt."

"Well, you do rise like a trout to the fly!"

Gena knew a sense of urgency. The best thing she could possibly do was change the subject. Get off the strictly personal, though she knew a passionate desire to continue the attack.

"You fly your own plane?" she asked with a complete volte-face.

He nodded his head, his gleaming eyes acknowledging such a glaring red herring. "I do, Miss Landon. A necessary adjunct to my way of life. I'm sure young Carson filled you in with a few salient details."

"He did say you owned a cattle station out West." There was an underlying tension now between them that could not be talked into non-existence.

"How far out West have you been?" he asked, mock casual.

"Not at all, I'm afraid." Even to her own ears her voice sounded apologetic. He had that effect on one. "I've seen about three thousand miles of the coastline from North Queensland to just past Melbourne on various motoring trips. But up until now I've always been a typical fringe dweller. It's a big country!"

"It is indeed," he agreed lazily. "But you've plenty of time, little one. You've never really felt the mood of the continent, heard its beating heart, until you've spent some time in the Outback. The uncanny relationship between the flora and the fauna and the natural landscape is quite fascinating. Like a giant tapestry ... rare and strangely off beat. There's nowhere I'd sooner be, and I've been just about everywhere!"

"Lucky you!" Gena smiled, surprised and moved by the depth of feeling in his voice. "I might see a little of the Outback sooner than you think. I have an uncle who owns quite a big property out in the Central West. You may know of him."

"Very likely, if he's in cattle," Cyrus Brandt agreed laconically. "What's his name?"

"Raff Cunningham. Raff for Raphael, I believe." She sat up quickly as they missed their turning. "Oh, I'm sorry, I thought you knew. You seemed so sure of the way. It was the last turn on the left."

He reversed the car swiftly. "My mistake!" he said in an odd sort of drawl. "I must have been paying a little too much attention to what you were saying. You're full of surprises, Miss Landon. And how would you be related to this Raff Cunningham?"

"Through my mother," she explained. "*Her* mother's brother, actually, so that makes him a great-uncle, doesn't it? The connection was broken when my mother died. I've almost decided to write to him. I can't think why I haven't before. My life took a different turning, I suppose."

"Perhaps it may come full circle. The element of chance plays a large part in controlling our destinies." His dark profile looked a little forbidding, but perhaps it was a trick of the light, for his voice was mild enough.

With mingled relief and disappointment, Gena saw her street-sign loom up. "The next turn to the right," she announced, her eyes big as lakes. "About six houses down. There's a jacaranda in bloom in front of it."

The big car slid into the pit of darkness under the jacaranda while blossoms fell over the bonnet like a shower. The moon glittered. All was curiously still except for the poignant call of a night bird. There was no crush of leaves underfoot, but their musky scent was on the air. Gena felt her heart leap into her throat. For a moment she was speechless, lost in a floating, threatening dream world.

He looked at the delicate oval of her face, her eyes suddenly glowing like sunlight on ice.

"You'd better go in, my child." He spoke gently, finally.

"I'm *not* your child!" she said in a sudden tantrum. How distressing to be so easily dismissed!

"Unfortunately not. I'd have had you over my knee long ago. Clearly someone needs to take a strong line with you." He reached past her waist to open the door, but she pushed his hand aside.

"Don't bother, I'm going. Good-bye, Mr. Brandt. One doesn't meet a cattle baron every day, but I could have forgone the opportunity."

"Is that so!" He was amused by her tone, young and arrogant. "Lies are their own punishment, Gena."

Her slender back was half turned to him as she fumbled for the door catch. Where on earth was it hidden?

Low laughter broke from him. "Patience opens all doors, try to remember it." His warm breath stirred the tendrils that curled at her ears. "Give up, Gena. You've lost the battle, but perhaps not the war!"

She shivered with instant comprehension and he caught her under the chin and tipped her head back to lie against his shoulder. She felt suddenly giddy, hemmed in by the sensual warmth of the night.

"Frightened?" the black velvet voice mocked her. "Poor little girl!"

"Not in the least!" She lay back, her eyes wide open, suspended, disorientated with this baffling, tormenting man she didn't yet know.

"I certainly never meant to touch you," he taunted her gently. "In fact I've no idea how you've come to be in my arms."

"Let me go, then," she whispered.

"Why should I? Even the moon has its dark side, Gena." He felt her tremble.

"But you're a stranger," she persisted with quiet desperation. "I dislike to repeat the obvious, but you're altogether a stranger."

"Hardly an irreversible statement, and in any case irrevelant." His thumb caressed the hollow in her throat. She saw the tawny eyes, the heavy lids, the deeply cleft chin, and something within her seemed to uncoil. She tried to turn her head away, but her body lost its independent power of movement. She arched her long throat and he caught her pulsing red mouth with his own.

"Oh no!"

The moon plummeted down, trailing fire. There was a moment of swirling darkness ... then gold dust falling from the sky ... cascades of gold dust, ringing them round. There was no yesterday, no today, no tomorrow. Nothing in the whole wide world existed, only surrender and a long, long enchantment. She felt as though she had been in his arms many times before. She knew every angle of that hard, vibrant body. It was a puzzle. Such a puzzle! And a sweetness. An intolerable sweetness! He was turning her heart over. Didn't he know it? Her trembling increased and she was free of him, reeling between a dream state and reality.

His hand retained a silken strand of her hair. "I hope you don't kiss every stranger like that, Gena."

Anger fought exultation. The fire that had blazed in her died.

"You've only yourself to blame," she said unsteadily. Her head was swimming, and her heart felt as if it would leap from her breast. Something akin to hostility stirred in her voice. "It's obvious that you're a past master in the art of seduction."

His hand tangled rather painfully in her hair. "Is that what you thought I was doing? Trying to seduce you? I would have started a great deal earlier in the evening. I have to fly out at five."

A shimmering mist hung before her eyes. Her graceful body tensed. "I'm sure that's never worried you before." She looked straight at him, hopelessly overwrought.

His powerful shoulders moved ironically. "Perhaps not. But schoolgirls rather trouble my conscience. They're too young, too helpless, too charming."

"Oh dear, oh dear, oh dear!" Gena pressed her long, beautiful fingers against her temples. The whole situation was beyond her. Cyrus Brandt was completely out of her league. Like a dangerous creature of the wild. Then there was the terrible weight of longing to be back in his arms again. What madness! Gena remained silent. She felt her emotions too transparent, too violent. She lowered her eyes as if in a trance.

He studied her silently, noting the pearly pallor to her skin. "Well, Sleeping Beauty?" He moved then, suddenly decisive. They were out of the car and he was holding her elbow, firmly, steadyingly. His voice was gently ironic. "What a pity you have this vulnerable quality. It makes you very dangerous. Good night, little one. I wouldn't have missed meeting you for the world."

The sultry air was filled with the fragrance of a thousand flowers, but Gena felt a coldness growing steadily in her. By now he was probably regretting his accidental surrender to impulse. A man like Cyrus Brandt would always find conquest easy. Hadn't she known it the moment she laid eyes on him? It would be fascinating to have so much power over women she thought with a sense of outrage. Yet the woman who cared for him would be clamped in chains, bound for ever to the dominant male and with so much boundless vitality! What a fate!

She moved her head languorously like a top-heavy chrysanthemum. Oh, to be as sexless as a flower! There was a thrilling, far more exciting world than she had ever supposed. And Cyrus Brandt had to show it to her! What a pity! A pity beyond all telling!

"Aren't you going to say good night to me?" The dark head was bent over her, his voice a thread of mockery on the night. "It's always for the lady to end a tête-à-tête."

Pride surged back like the tide. The most precious, saving pride.

"*Not* goodnight. It's good*bye*, Mr. Brandt." She spoke with impeccable dignity, but her body, that traitor, betrayed her. He made a slight movement towards her and she shied away from him like a startled filly.

He laughed suddenly, a flickering glow around his uncanny irises. "You're wrong about that, Gena," he said with peculiar emphasis, and turned away without another word.

Gena walked up to the house like a waif out of a dark dream. A kind of angry shame burned in her. In the space of a few moments her life had moved into another cycle. *And now there was no return!* The words seemed to swirl in the soft, purplish air. Her eyes burned with unshed tears and they would have to remain unshed. Linda would be certain to be awake wanting to know how the evening went ... what Tony did ... what Tony said ... *Who was Tony?* She would have to concoct a long story to keep Linda happy ... fabricate the latter part of the evening with a vengeance.

Men like Cyrus Brandt didn't normally swim into a woman's ken. She only hoped she would never lay eyes on him again. She had no intention of being tossed up like driftwood on the sand. Such a man was made of dangerous stuff! The male scent of him clung to her and she accepted his enormous impact on her with fatalistic resignation.

45

A young man not yet; an older man not at all! She turned the words over in her mind, woman-like lost in the vividness of her resentment. Cyrus Brandt was welcome to his precious freedom. Pity the woman to unleash the demon in him! though some might not be able to resist the temptation. Like the redhead! Innocents, like herself, would do well to beware of him.

Hours later she was still tossing and turning, seeking oblivion. There was the most peculiar roar in her ears like the roar of the surf. Gena sat up in bed in the moonlight, two silvery braids swinging over her shoulders, her eyes wide and sleepless in the pale oval of her face.

She could not be calm about the events of the night. A fever burned in her. Her chin sank on to her knees and a forceful dark face glimmered before her. Her eyes, surprising a secret, lit with an inner glow, her mouth ached in remembered ecstasy. She fell back on the pillows with a muffled cry. Her reactions were quite incomprehensible to her. Could it be she was frightened of a real, full-blooded emotional affair?

Gena slipped into an uneasy sleep, only to dream herself in a rain forest, stalked by a cougar!

CHAPTER III

SATURDAY'S party promised to be highly successful and in a final fling of good spirits Gena decided to accept Tony's persistent telephoned apologies. He was charmingly abject, swore to trade in the Mustang for a Mini-Minor and by a singularly fortunate chance, professed himself to be free for the party. Gena hung up laughing.

Encouraged by the brilliant weather, the smallish dinner party had developed into a largish barbecue and pool party. There were hordes of people who wanted to come and half of them seemed to have house guests who just could not be left, so one way and another the party grew and grew!

By eight o'clock, a gay, informally dressed crowd swarmed over the house and patio area, laughing, chatting, ready to enjoy themselves. The house bloomed with lights and flowers and stood up well to the professional scrutiny of Paul Landon's colleagues. Peeping over the staircase, Linda battled with panic. She felt more like an apprehensive neurotic than a hopeful party-giver. Yet it was so much easier to have people moving about freely than to suffer the enforced oppression of a formal dinner party. How she suffered at those parties. How Paul and Gena shone!

Thinking of them both, Linda found she had the courage to come on down. Strange to think she had once taken dictation impeccably. It's a wonder I was able to do that, she thought with characteristic self-deprecation. Only an hour ago in their room Paul had told her how much he loved her and how pretty she looked, and she hugged the memory to herself. Gena, so chic herself, had added unstinting admiration of the new outfit, so what was wrong with her? Linda's knees still shook beneath the skirt of her jersey silk hostess gown. She smoothed a self-conscious hand over it. It was really quite beautiful in all the "iridescent blues and greens of the ocean", as Paul put it, and it did wonderful things for her eyes, so why was she cursed with this extra-sensitive nature? Other women less pretty lived exceptionally full, varied lives, blessed with social expertise. Ah well! Linda went on down.

In the spacious terrazzo-floored entrance hall Gena was greeting a wave of new arrivals and Linda felt her spirits waver. Lucky Gena to have so much poise and humour. And Gena was her mother all over again, though she did get her long beautiful limbs from her father, for Virginia had been petite. Virginia! Even the unspoken name caused Linda pain. She tried to be rational about it, but she was too much in love, too plagued with self-doubt to succeed. It wasn't that she was jealous. No, never that! How could one be jealous of such a young, tragic ghost? But with Gena constantly in front of her, so glowing, so vital, so spirited in her manner, Virginia could never really die for anyone. Sometimes Linda thought she surprised an expression on her husband's face, as he looked at his daughter, that could only be remembrances of things past. Flashes of Virginia . . . her laugh, the dancing points of light in her eyes; those piquant eyes that gave Gena's face so much of its character.

Linda walked towards them, ice-bound in her shyness, her deep-rooted aversion to social gatherings. Gena swung round and saw her and came swiftly forward to take her arm.

'Lindy darling, do come and meet Dr. and Mrs. Porter! They've just been telling me they're enchanted with our lovely home!'

Linda went forward smiling, her nerves stretched unbearably, for all her unhurried manner. Mrs. Porter looked a terrifyingly perfect woman, with an inexhaustible supply of small talk. Gena, feeling her freezing, rubbed Linda's arm affectionately, trying to ease the strain out of her. A few minutes later, with Linda safe within the circle of her husband's arm, Gena hurried up to her room to recheck her appearance. There had been so many last-minute details to attend to that she hardly knew if she had her lipstick on straight. Loving parties herself, Linda's attitude nevertheless affected her, causing a certain tension she would not normally have felt. She leaned nearer the mirror, rather liking the bright colour in her cheeks. Excitement, of course! Her outfit was brand new. Dashing – pure and simple! A four-piece linen ensemble in lacquer red comprising a tiny cropped jacket and flared trousers over its own matching bikini. Gena patted her bare golden midriff complacently and went on downstairs, her silken hair gleaming. The massed gold of chrysanthemums looked well under a huge abstract she had completed a year ago. She had called it, rather fancifully, "The Eye of Summer" and her father, no doubt biased, had declared it of considerable merit and insisted on hanging it in the entrance hall. Gena had to admit that it suited the room in scale and mood; a glowing, swirling pattern of interlocking sharp yellows and greens with touches of the brilliant blue of a tropical sky. She gave it another critical glance, then looked into the crowded living-room. From behind her firm hands came up to grasp her bare shoulders.

"My little darling, I am here at last!"

Gena swung, bright-eyed and amused. "Hello, Tony!"

His dark eyes flamed under her slow, sweet smile. "Beauty and riches within my grasp!"

She looked up at him. "You really are very quick!"

"Tenacious too. Then you're the kind of girl men can't ignore."

"Heavens! I'll have to do something about it."

"Never change a winning game," Tony breathed in her ear. "Come dance with me, sweet." He turned and led her out on to the terrace. Sweet, throbbing music from a muted stereogram spilled out to them.

"What a wonderful night!" Tony matched his steps to hers. "Delicious with the scent of summer, youth, and innocence." He held her away from him, his dark eyes gleaming. "Innocence, pet?"

"You see what you see!" Gena surveyed him with cool amusement fighting the tiny traitorous wish that he was someone else. Someone very tall, very dark, very devastating in the wild dark. Her mind closed down on her storm-filled remembrances.

Tony's eyes sharpened, his senses acute. "What's up? You look different. Very Mona Lisa-wise."

"Really! I thought I was my usual calmly demented self."

Tony's arm tightened. "Don't toy with me, doll. You *are* different, so lose the cryptic smile. You wouldn't by any chance be hankering after the cattle baron, would you?"

Gena lifted the warm silky weight of her hair off her nape, mildly astonished at his perception.

"You're crazy!"

"The hell I am. A lie is always an easy answer, angel. Don't think I haven't used them in the past."

"You're crazy all right!" Gena repeated. "Now don't annoy me, Tony, with awkward questions. We're not embroiled in a love affair."

"Aren't we? In that case you'd better simmer down and take no notice of me. I'm ripe for round the bend, anyway. And you're the cause of it. You know that?"

Gena's fringed eyes darkened. "You're very adept at a flirtation."

He dipped his dark head and nipped her ear. "Who said anything about a flirtation? I'm deadly serious."

Gena struggled to keep a flippant mind. She turned her head, seeking a change of subject. "There are heaps of men in my life, allowing for a little poetic licence, but isn't that Raye Newell who just came in?"

Tony swivelled quickly and a startled exclamation fell from his lips.

"Lumme, it is! And just look at her outfit! One step short of sheer bad taste." He snorted in amusement. "I never thought she'd have the nerve to put anything like that on."

Gena studied the offending tube of white crêpe, marvellously slashed at neckline and thigh. "Well, it does go a little further than suggestion," she said candidly, then immediately regretted it. "She does have a lovely figure, though," she pointed out fairly.

Tony drew back, amazed. "God, it's not a patch on yours! You are a paragon of all the virtues, aren't you, sweetie? For the first time I'm beginning to doubt your interest in me. I don't mind telling you Raye Newell has been after me for God knows how long." He sighed elaborately. "I can't really say at this minute how long I'll be able to hold out."

Gena laughed, dancing points of light in her eyes.

"Why try?"

Tony sobered. "You *know* why, dearest, and this is not the prelude to an old routine." His strong young arms tightened and Gena knew a strong impulse for flight. He was getting far too serious. From now on the going would be tough! She moved swiftly out of his arms.

"Do please excuse me, Tony. I can see Linda hovering. She must need a hand."

Tony gazed back at her cynically. "Slipped like a fish from the net! Do you know, pet, I just may console myself with that dear little dolly bird over there – the one in her limpid little gymslip."

"Do that," Gena laughed. "I bet she'll be bowled over from the first minute." She moved away from him, smiling with airy sweetness.

"How blind I've been! It all fits. You *don't* love me."

"We might swim together later," she promised. "Now I really must go."

Watching her, Tony thought even her heavy sweep of

hair danced with life. He resisted the impulse to go after her and encircle that taut golden midriff. But he'd get her complete attention yet. The past few days he'd been busy . . . very busy . . . checking out one Cyrus Brandt. Gena would be most definitely interested in his findings. *And* disillusioned, if he knew Gena. Cyrus Brandt was *that* kind of man!

For all that Gena found she had very little time for the proposed swim before supper. Young, lithe bodies kept striking the water, creating a fascinating spectacle of light and limb. But Gena was unable to join them. She circled back across the patio with a tray of drinks and a few of the crowd sang out to her. She waved a hand but continued on to the kitchen. From previous entertaining she and Linda had found Italian dishes very popular and Linda's *cannelloni*, a huge casserole of pasta tubes filled with ground beef, spices and finely chopped spinach, and topped with a rich tomato cheese sauce, needed last-minute reheating. The individually baked pizzas were Gena's contribution as well as a luscious Sicilian cassata of layered pound cake filled with a cream cheese and candied fruit mixture, and covered with chocolate frosting. Almost from the arrival of the first Italian migrant Italian cooking had found a firm place in Australian kitchens, and Gena and Linda were addicted to it. Supper at Landons' was expected to be on the sumptuous side as a matter of course, and this reputation kept both women busy for the best part of that morning and a full half hour before supper. With the buffet tables laid and the candles and flower arrangements placed, Gena went in search of her father. She found him emerging, head down, from his study. Gena shivered involuntarily, sensing that the next few minutes would reveal a great deal to her. Her father looked up to see her, a little pale under his summer tan.

"There you are, dear. I've just had a call from a Mrs. Edna Carroll. The weight of my years has suddenly fallen upon me. She was Raff Cunningham's housekeeper for the past five years."

"He's dead, Dad. Is that it?" Gena addressed her father directly.

"Yes, darling. Three o'clock this afternoon. The old fellow's been ailing for some time now. He must have been well over eighty. Poor old chap, I can't think how he ever dropped out of our lives. He adored your mother." Paul Landon nibbled on his underlip. "You know, I feel quite badly about this."

"I feel rather sad myself. When's the funeral?"

"Monday afternoon. One of us will have to go – a very belated gesture, I know. Mrs. Carroll is leaving Melaleuca almost immediately. She's going to live with her sister in Townsville. She sounded fed-up. I gather there's been a bit of trouble. Other than that I couldn't get a word out of her. She measures out her words a few at a time."

While her father was talking Gena was already working out her plans.

"I'll go, Dad," she said decisively. "To the funeral, I mean."

"*You*, dear?" her father gave her a doubtful look. "You know *you* haven't the time. I'll fly out, of course. I might even take some time off, see a little of the Outback while I'm at it. I might even be able to stay at the house."

"But would you want to, dear?" Her father glanced at her in surprise.

Gena didn't hesitate. "Why not? Even if it's haunted it would be by a kindly old ghost."

"There's a point. But really . . ." Paul Landon checked himself. "Oh, never mind, I really don't know what I'm trying to say anyway."

Gena's thoughts were flowing. "Who'll get it, I wonder – the property?"

Her father pursed his lips, slightly bemused.

"I don't really know. It could even be you. The old fellow was short on relations, so far as I know. But no doubt he found someone of whom he was particularly fond." He passed a hand over his dark head in a familiar gesture. "I feel I should go with you. It's a bad time for me with the Doyle contract, but still –! "

Gena broke in on him. "You know you can't. Besides, it won't matter a scrap to poor old Uncle Raff. I seem to remember him faintly. He had very blue eyes." Suddenly her own eyes filled with tears and her father moved towards her, putting an arm around her.

"You're a good girl, Gena. I wish I could suggest Linda's going with you, but the whole business would only upset her. She'd be out of her depth. In any case, we won't say anything about this until the morning. Then we'll make plans." He shot back his cuff. "What time's supper?"

"In a few minutes. That's what I came to tell you. Everyone should be out of the pool and dried off. I think they're all enjoying themselves. Oh dear, what a night!" she breathed half dejectedly.

"Buck up now, dear," her father said, patting her shoulder. "It was bound to happen sooner or later – the sad normal course of life. The old chap had a good innings after all. It will do no good to brood. Now let's go in before we're missed."

True to his word, Tony cornered Gena for supper. Talking non-stop between numerous mouthfuls, he ate chicken in aspic with uninhibited enjoyment and urged Gena to do the same.

Gena found she had little appetite. She sipped at this, nibbled at that, picked up her cassata and put it down again. She looked over the buffet tables, deriving a certain satisfaction from the single-minded determination of their guests to make a clean sweep of their contents.

Tony whispered in her ear, "Let's take a romantic trip into the garden."

"Not on your life."

"It's settled, then," Tony said comfortably, and tucked her arm beneath his own. "How long is it since I met you? Six weeks . . . seven? And to think all this time I've been fighting my passion for you!" Gena laughed and he bent near her, his voice freighted with urgency. "Say there's no one else!"

"Heavens, Tony, you're not serious," Gena said sharply. "You sound just like a melodrama – unrequited love, broken hearts, faded flowers, a bunch of old letters. I have no time for a love affair. I'm free-lancing now. It keeps me busy."

"Wonderful! Then we can be married right away."

"But we can't."

Tony looked at her. "Why, for goodness' sake? Why?"

"Chiefly because I don't want to. You must take my feelings into account."

Tony was silent and Gena had the feeling that he was terribly disappointed, but he merely cleared his throat, a gleam in his eyes.

"Take a good look at yourself, Gena Landon, spinster, twenty-two. You'll change your mind. I'm suave, polished, courteous, assured, self-effacing or helpful. I have the stamina of a camel, and the interesting thing about me is that I don't give up easily."

Despite herself Gena burst out laughing. "I agree you're very versatile, but I don't love you, Tony, and I must tell you so. I'm sorry if I haven't reacted as sweetly as I should."

Tony tipped a finger to her lips. "Hush, hush, sweet Gena. Let's look at the garden. It's beautiful. Irregular, natural, the way a garden should be."

"You'll have to come over and help me weed it," she said lightly, forgetting her earlier resolution not to give him any further encouragement. Two garden lamps stood up like spears in the moonlight, tinging her face with gold. Tony's eyes softened as though contemplating a dream. He took hold of Gena's shoulders, pressing them soulfully. "I'm not sure if you're not the most beautiful girl in the world."

"Thank you, Tony. Always the graceful liar."

He shook his head. "I swear it's the truth. But that's not what I got you out here for."

Gena gave an elaborate start. "My curiosity is rapidly

turning to alarm. What *is* it you got me out here for? In earshot of my father, I might add."

"Oh, to demolish a dream," Tony said suddenly, slyly, twisting sideways. "The cattle baron, who else!" he remarked with the air of producing an impressive but improbable white rabbit.

"Won't you sit down?" Gena indicated a garden seat a few feet away. The air was almost heady, redolent with the scented splendour of frangipani. Tony sat on the edge of the seat, drawing Gena down with him.

"You may not have heard this, dear . . ."

"I've a feeling I will soon."

". . . but the cattle baron's up to his neck in intrigue . . . woman troubles . . . land-grabbing schemes, the lot!"

"Cyrus Brandt?" Gena's voice indicated that she was ready to believe anything.

Again Tony's eyes gleamed. "The same one. These past few days I've been busy. A very busy boy checking him out."

Gena felt her conscience protest. "Sure it's unethical to pry into private files, let alone discuss a client with an outsider."

"There, I knew you'd be interested," Tony said, not at all abashed. "Just when you needed a bit of life, too."

Gena sat upright and Tony looked pleased. "You look very professional, dear."

"It's surprising how much pain I get when I move," she said dryly, covering a very real sense of heartache. "Do tell me, Tony. I know you're dying to, and I've had such a remarkably uneventful life myself."

"Me too! But give me the glamour boys any day," Tony

58

said, and began to whistle softly through his teeth. "It's like this, dear. The redhead, believe it or not, is the sister-in-law. And a widow! Picture it to yourself. The husband, Brandt's younger brother, was killed in a car smash eight months ago. There's a child, a little girl, and there's some speculation as to whose little girl it is."

Gena stood up. "Well, really, Tony, I'm not *that* interested. You make me feel like a voyeur."

Tony ignored her, pulling her down again. "*She* was Keera Hyland, the spoilt rotten only daughter of old Josh Hyland, the millionaire grazier, financier and part-time philanthropist. I have here in my left-hand pocket an engagement photo taken some ten years ago, which you may study at your leisure . . . no, don't grab, dear . . . of one Keera Hyland . . . and wait for it . . . the dashingly handsome Cyrus Brandt. For reasons as yet unknown to me, the engagement was broken off and two years later the beauteous Keera married the younger brother, a few years her junior, but quite pleased with the deal. A child is born. Come a few years exit the husband. Widow and child are now ensconced at Bauhinia, which, dear girl . . . and now I come to my *coup de grâce* . . . borders Melaleuca, the property of one Raphael Cunningham." Gena started and Tony patted her hand and continued, "Brandt, the big wheeler-dealer, has been negotiating the sale of other properties adjoining his own – always tricky in the early stages, but it appears he wants Melaleuca, run-down though it may be. The old man won't sell out. Not for love nor money."

And not even that, Gena thought sadly. "And all this you've discovered through Cyrus Brandt's *confidential*
59

chats with your father?"

Tony looked amazed, unable to gauge her new mood, the reasons behind it. "My poor Gena," he said sympathetically, "it's been a shock for you. I blame myself. Though I would have blamed myself more if I hadn't put you wise about the cattle baron. You said yourself that he looked like a gentleman adventurer. And who knows, you just could run into him again, if you trip off to your uncle's. Forewarned is forearmed, so they say."

Gena debated in silence whether to disclose her own "coup", then decided against it. Let him find out the hard way!

From under the bamboos a young woman slinked towards them. *Slinked* was the only word for it, Gena decided dispassionately. It was Raye Newell, the inveterate seductress.

"Dare I interrupt this intimate little scene?" she asked with saccharine sweetness. "Wedding bells can't be too far off."

"It takes more than a cosy set-up to set the bells tolling," Gena retorted in a voice brilliantly designed to indicate that she couldn't care less.

Raye gave her a long glance and transferred her attention to Tony. "Dance with me, lover."

"And what makes you think I *can*?" Tony smiled rather sardonically.

Raye seemed taken back by her own boldness. "What's wrong with you?"

"Oh, nothing," Tony shrugged. "I'm just feeling sorry for myself."

Raye treated Gena to another of her all-seeing glances.

"With good reason, I'm sure."

Tony got up with a backward, "What did I tell you" expression. "Come on, Raye, now's your chance to live a little," he drawled in his sexier-than-thou voice.

The last thing Gena heard was Raye's laugh, rippling merrily. She probably hopes my heart has been stirred to jealousy, Gena thought, her mind in a torment. And it *has*! But Tony had nothing to do with it. She got up slowly from the seat, realising with a pang that the evening had gone dead on her.

Hours later, when every last guest had gone home and every last glass and ashtray had been collected, Gena hurried up to her room. She closed the door, crossed to the bed and threw herself on it. Now I'll cry and cry, she thought to herself. I'll cry and cry and cry. But she was wrong about that. No tears gathered and she twisted from side to side, but her face only got hot. She was too mad to cry. Cyrus Brandt, that scheming land shark, womaniser, and God knows what else, had made a fool of her. Treated her like a wanton child. Deceived her wilfully. Oh yes, they would meet again! He made no mistake about that.

She lay there fuming, planning a line of campaign. Before she was finished Cyrus Brandt would listen respectfully while she spoke. Not every woman was fair game, she reminded herself, while her breast rose and fell like a tropical sea. When tears came to her eyes they were for a shadowy figure called Raff Cunningham. How strange that she should have grown up with such remarkably little curiosity about her mother's favourite uncle. In those days, her father had reared her with a judicious mixture of love and discipline and a singular unwillingness to share her with anyone. But tonight for some reason Gena felt very close to old Uncle Raff. He had visited them a few times in her childhood, offering to take Gena at holiday time. He swore she would be well looked after. But nothing ever came of it. Her father, deprived of a beloved wife, could hardly bear to part with the child. Now Gena determined she would see Melaleuca, if only the once. Ironic that it should border Bauhinia. She tried to sort out her feelings about its disturbing owner, but she couldn't come to grips with the problem. The whole business was too uncanny, like the interwoven threads of fate.

She lay there motionless, plotting whole conversations where she invariably came out on top. Sleep came hard that night!

CHAPTER IV

Sunshine blazed into the small office and through the windows came fresh, clean air. Raphael Cunningham's solicitor drew a funny face in the corner of his blotter put a pair of horns on it and looked at Gena from over the tops of his glasses. His heavy, rather humorous face fell into mournful lines, like a saddened bloodhound.

"Can't say how sorry I am, Miss Landon. Raff Cunnigham was a grand old chap. One of the Outback's real old characters. A pioneer in his day with plenty of say in these parts. 'Course, he got pretty eccentric towards the end, as a big man's entitled to do, I guess. Thought everyone was tryin' to shift him off his land. Took it mighty hard."

"And weren't they?" Gena's eyes sparkled. Tom Wiggins noticed the sparkle, but missed the astringent touch.

"Well," he considered at length, "I won't say the old fellow didn't have plenty of offers. Melaleuca is in a very strategic position. Not far from the Junction. The junction of four creeks and the river, that is. Yes, sir, he had offers all right. Offers he'd have been mad to refuse."

Glena sat up very straight. "Money's not everything, Mr. Wiggins. My great-uncle was well over eighty. He was born on Melaleuca and he was perfectly entitled to die on it. In fact I'd have been surprised if he wanted anything else. There must be a point in your life when money has no value. Uncle Raff wasn't meant to end his days in a four-roomed apartment in the city."

Tom Wiggins was following her line of reason with painful intensity. "No, ma'am, of course not. I didn't mean to imply any such thing. But the property was too big for him. Overrun by pear in parts, and that manager feller! . . . well, he wasn't making much of a fist of things. Not as if the seasons have been bad either, or there was no permanent water on it. Why, Bauhinia across the junction . . ."

Gena jumped up quickly, almost capsizing her chair. "I didn't come here to listen to Mr Cyrus Brandt's success story, staggering though that may be. My uncle may not have been a good business man, but he was a good cattle man, surely?"

Tom Wiggins was looking at her as if he was beginning to suspect she was more than a little like her uncle. "In his day, little lady. In his day. Now sit down," he said soothingly. "You've got yourself all hot and bothered, and for no good reason. It's my duty to point out a few of the drawbacks regarding your inheritance. Melaleuca is badly in need of hard work, but I'm pleased to tell you there's no overdraft on the property."

They both turned at a noise in the room behind them. The glass door swung open and the moon-faced teenager Gena had passed on her way into the inner sanctum wheeled in a tea trolley. She smiled excitedly at Gena, examining her face, her clothes, right down to her shoes. No detail, to be stored away for subsequent retelling, was missed.

Gena smiled back, rather touched by her interest.

"Hope it's weak enough," Patsy breathed surprisingly.

64

"Thank you, Patsy," Tom Wiggins exclaimed warmly, and waved a large hand with a pleasant but dismissive gesture.

Patsy backed out of the room, like a puppet on a string, eyeing Gena until the last. Gena turned back to the tea trolley. It was set with a fine lace cloth, a silver teapot and milk jug and surprisingly delicate china. A huge pile of sultana scones dripping golden butter sat on a doiley. Gena gave them an apprehensive glance and looked at Mr. Wiggins.

"Shall I pour?"

"Please do. There's nothing I like better than tea and scones," he commented unnecessarily. "The wife made these specially in your honour."

"They look lovely," Gena murmured, now committed to eating her share. The solicitor accepted his tea with a pleasant nod, tipping his chair to a nicely calculated angle.

"I don't imagine a pretty young lady like yourself will want to be away long from the bright lights, but there is the term of residence to consider. The property is yours, of course, lock, stock and barrel, just so long as you reside on it for a period of six months starting from as soon as practicable. That's the only stipulation your uncle made apart from terms of sale. In the very likely event of your wanting to dispose of the property you may not on any account sell out to Brandt Enterprises or any affiliated agency. I must stress that point. It's very clear in the will. Your uncle was carrying on a sort of feud with Cy . . . Mr. Brandt, that is. They were very close at one time!" Tom Wiggins put his fragile cup down with a resounding thud. "Now if you want my opinion –"

"I take it you're an admirer of Mr. Brandt's?" Gena pressed him into the admission.

Tom Wiggins eyebrows shot up. "Who isn't? Cyrus Brandt is a big man in this State and the all-powerful name around here. A fine bloke, I can tell you. A straight shooter and approachable too, which is more'n I can say for a lot with only a quarter of his money."

But he doesn't charm everyone, Gena thought fiercely. Aloud she commented, "There's no doubt he has a few things going for him." She blinked away her vivid recollections of them.

Tom Wiggins looked at her uncertainly. "Well now, Miss Landon, I think that covers everything. If not, I'm always at your disposal." He looked over at her and smiled. "I'd be happy to run you back to the property just whenever you're ready. It's a good sixty miles, and I guess you're tired after the funeral and all. Sure was a big one – one of the finest send-offs I've seen in forty years out West. 'Course, everyone was mighty curious to see the new owner. Never guessed it would be such a beautiful young lady. Next thing you know, you'll be married off, if you stay long enough. We've some very determined matchmaking mothers. A good-looking woman is highly prized out West, and when she has a little something in the bank to go with it –!" Tom Wiggins winked expressively.

Gena digested all this in silence, then she smiled. She had to. She picked up her handbag and stood up.

"I'm ready when you are, Mr. Wiggins. I only have to collect my baggage from the hotel."

"Nice of you to call it that," Tom Wiggins smiled

widely, then paused to give Gena's chic little black suit a doubtful glance. "Perhaps you'd like to change out of your funeral clothes," he suggested tactfully.

Not for the first time that day Gena tried to maintain her composure. A few hours before, seated in the front pew of the little bush church, she had, to her consternation, experienced the highly inappropriate desire to laugh. The service was conducted by a tall, very homespun clergyman who suffered from hay fever, and his sincere little tribute to the memory of Raphael Cunningham, one-time parishioner, was interspersed with a volley of sneezes. No one, apart from Gena, seemed to see anything comical in it. Indeed her silent shaking had been taken for a very proper expression of grief.

Outside in the deluge of sunshine Gena turned to wave to Patsy, who hung like a possum from an upper window, then she followed Tom Wiggins' determined lead. A smooth cultured drawl brought them both up short.

"Well, if it isn't the big city belle!"

Gena spun in a trice. "If it isn't the cattle baron," she retorted, keeping her voice steady. He stood there regarding her with the same arrogant appraisal that had made her so uncomfortable the first time they met. There was amusement and something else in the gold-flecked eyes. He turned to the older man, giving Gena time to get a hold on herself. How could a man contrive to be elegant in jeans, high boots, a pale blue shirt carelessly buttoned and a pearl grey Stetson? She dragged her eyes off the man.

"How's business, Tom?" she heard him say smoothly.

Tom Wiggins' face lit up. "Real brisk, Cy, and that's

a fact. I'm just taking Miss Landon here out to her property. I guess most everyone knows old Raff had that certain niece somewheres."

"I guess they did," the cattle baron agreed dryly, narrowing his eyes against the sunlight. "Anyway, I can take over that chore for you. I'm on my way back to Bauhinia. The jeep is down the road."

Gena's "Please don't bother!" cut across Tom Wiggins' "That's well, then!" Gena shrugged her slim shoulders philosophically and gave herself up to the inevitable.

"Thank you, Mr. Brandt," she managed with excessive politeness. "I hope I didn't give you the wrong impression."

Cyrus Brandt shrugged off her sarcasm, though his eyes were gleaming.

"No need to ask you two if you know each other." Tom Wiggins looked from one to the other, beaming.

"From way back!" the cattle baron announced laconically, causing him to go up even further in Tom Wiggins' estimation. Cyrus Brandt never had been known to miss a trick.

"Well now, I'll cut back to the office, then," the older man's face broke into a delighted smile. "Sure has been a pleasure meeting you, ma'am, and just remember I'm at your service for any little thing."

Gena gave him her transforming smile that lit up her face. "Thank you, Mr. Wiggins, and you're very welcome to call out to Melaleuca. Please don't leave it to business."

Tom Wiggins blushed hotly and the cattle baron's eyes glittered.

"See you, then, Tom," he murmured pleasantly, and

took hold of Gena's shoulder, propelling her across the quite deserted road.

"You'd better get rid of that outfit, honey. You look as improbable as a lily on a claypan," he observed dryly.

Gena looked straight ahead. "That's rather a loose characterisation, isn't it, Mr. Brandt? I've always thought it unfair to classify people. Actually I'm an outdoor girl!"

The burnished glance slicked over her and came to rest on the gleaming artful coils of her hair.

"You don't look too woodsy to me!"

"I am, I assure you. I've spent plenty of time in the garden and I've even been known to take long walks!"

"You might find yourself *running* here," the cattle baron drawled slowly, and suddenly laughed.

"What's so amusing?" She tilted her face up to him unwillingly.

"*You*, Miss Bristle Brush!" His eyes narrowed on the smooth golden oval of her face. "You don't even know what it's all about."

Gena looked away very abruptly. "Very likely. You're way out of my league."

"Natch-ur-ally!" A smile creased his cheeks, and he looked so devastatingly handsome she nearly choked in annoyance.

"If you wouldn't mind waiting," she announced crisply as they reached the verandah of the hotel.

He swept a deep salute with the pearl grey Stetson. "Take all the time you want, ma'am, but be ready to leave in ten minutes."

Gena spun on her heel, waiting until she was inside the

69

small vestibule before muttering a few irate words. How the man got her goat! She sped up the stairs and into her room, seeing her two neatly packed bags side by side. She opened up one swiftly and took out a pair of slacks in buttercup yellow with a matching silky knot and threw them down on the bed. Minutes later her black suit was neatly packed away and she was dressed and pulling at her sleek double chignon. Relieved of its confining pins, her hair swirled on to her shoulders in two gilded coils. There was a tap at the door and she turned to grope for her sandals, hastily buttoning her shirt. It was bound to be the boy for her bags. It wasn't. Cyrus Brandt lounged in the doorway, his Stetson tipped over his eyes.

"Your bags, lady," he drawled. "A sweet little thing like you couldn't be expected to carry them." He moved indolently across the threshold with his big cat tread and Gena backed on pure instinct. He was a big man and the room was far too small for both of them.

"I'm not *too* little!" she pointed out dryly. "In fact, not to put too fine a point on it, I'm not *little* at all. I'm well above average height."

The cattle baron examined her in detail, causing her to colour up hotly.

"Well, let's put it this way, you look *little* to me. Now, the bags, where are they?"

Gena pointed wordlessly, incapable of speech. She swept up her make-up and deposited it in her fringed suede bag, glanced into the spotted mirror and began to braid her hair for extra neatness.

Cyrus Brandt's reflection towered behind her in the mirror.

"Marvellous how a pigtail can change you back into a long-limbed brat."

"Thanks!" Gena looked haughtily back at him. "You may not realise it, Mr. Brandt, but I'm twenty-two, going on twenty-three."

"You'll be married before you make it," he retorted, his hands deep in his pockets.

"How absurd!" She knew a quick rise of sharpest excitement as his eyes met hers. Her delicate black brows arched imperiously. "My passion, no less intense than yours, is for *freedom*." It sounded just fine the way she said it.

"Fiddlesticks!" he replied inelegantly. "You're just quoting the militant liberation front. You were born to be loved. To be made love to ... and that for a woman means marriage. Some men might even find your beauty alone ample return."

Gena was breathing fast. She had restored order to her hair but no order at all to her thoughts. "I take it not *you*, Mr. Brandt," she said quickly, without making it a question.

He took a moment to consider. "No, not me, honey. Apart from anything else, you're too apt to fly off the handle – a very disconcerting habit in a woman. You'll have to work on that one."

Gena knew a fierce necessity to throw something. She stood there, her agitation marked.

"Come on now, don't fall into the scowling sulks. I'm quite unimpressed with female tantrums. Besides, a few home truths shouldn't throw a big city belle like you."

Gena tossed her head. "You've been the big wheel

71

around here far too long. All those mutterings of approval every time you appear – why, you're nothing but a . . . a . . . charming half-savage! " she brought out triumphantly.

He bowed ironically. "Including present company. Thank you, Miss Landon. Now what say we shove off before we come to blows? That would be most unladylike." He reached out with one fluid movement and picked up the bags, tucking one under his arm and gripping the other.

"Now, if he'll only trip! " Gena thought to herself, and slammed the door after them. But nothing like that happened. The cattle baron strode ahead of her with ease and grace while her sparkling eyes bored a hole between his broad, powerful shoulders. Unconsciously she registered that his hips looked very lean in comparison and she was forced to admit his quite extraordinary physical splendour. Her blood began racing and she detested herself for her weakness.

On the broken third stair, Gena lost balance. She grabbed for the railing, missed it and careered into the cattle baron. She knew a moment of rootlessness and panic, then he caught her, his hand biting into her narrow waist.

"A for effort! " he said lightly, "but don't try any more woman magic on me, honey. I thought I told you I was immune to satiny skin."

Gena blushed furiously. "How dismally dull for you! But even you could have too much of a good thing! "

His grip on her tightened, and she tried ineffectually to get away from him. "You know darn well I tripped! " she found herself saying, her skin tingling, an apricot glow on her cheekbones. She continued to struggle and he breathed near her ear,

"Now who's the savage?"

"You're hurting me, Mr. Brandt," she said sweetly, trying to outstare him, but the first fall of the eyes was hers.

He released her, his mouth twitching. "A restful manner is a big asset in a woman. Work on it, Gena, if you want to impress me."

She rubbed her waist tenderly. "Don't tell me, I know it. You're Leo, the sun sign. Fire and domination. Lashings of action . . . ambition . . . the worst kind of man!"

"Methinks the lady protests too much!" he drawled. "Now what would you be, Miss Bristle Brush? Gemini, I shouldn't wonder. Spirit and passion. Over fond of dramatics. Not enough balance. A pity, for it's one of my favourite signs."

Gena almost danced out on to the veranda. "You've *no* idea how patronising you are! It's horrible. Actually, *I'm* Leo."

He turned to smile at her, a real smile. "And I'm Aquarius – on the face of it not a bad combination. Just goes to show even the stars can go wrong. Now if you were a few years older and more docile I might be tempted to give the astrology bit a go just for the heck of it."

Gena broke into a run. Further down the street a jeep was parked. It was bound to be his. Cyrus Brandt came up after her. "Colour-matched in your honour," he jibbed carelessly. Gena had to laugh, for the jeep was a bright yellow with a black interlocking B.J. ringed in bronze.

He stowed the bags away and gave her a hand into the jeep before going around to the driver's side. He drove fast, in expert control of the vehicle. Gena sat back, saying nothing until they were clear of the town. Blue gums rushed at them and big shady paperbarks and through the gaps in the trees she could see the purple haze of the distant ranges. In the thick green grass daisies were closing their yellow-lined petals for the night, and even as she watched the air was suddenly full of leaves as a rose pink galah shot shrieking up to the sky. She threw it a glance of startled admiration and turned to the man at her side.

"You must have been one of the few people to miss the funeral," she said carefully, without expression. "*And you knew my uncle well, a fact you never saw fit to mention.*"

He flicked a glance at her classic profile. "I was wondering how long it would take you to get around to that. You're way overdue." He stared ahead for a few seconds, his dark face withdrawn. There was a curious awkward silence. "In any way I'm sorry about it," he said finally, "but I'm no hypocrite. Old Raff would have lynched me given half a chance."

Gena stared. "Surely you don't mean it?"

The topaz eyes gleamed pure mockery. "No, I'm just being humorous in my carefree way. The last time I saw him he was at the other end of a double-barrelled shotgun – blatant symptoms of inhospitality, wouldn't you say?"

Gena was gazing at him with her mouth slightly open, brooding, though she was not aware she was doing it.

He laughed rather grimly. "The truth is always better

74

than a pack of sentimental lies, my girl. Towards the end Raff Cunningham was probably the most unpredictable old character I've ever come across. God forgive me for speaking ill of the dead," he said, his dark face as arrogant as the devil.

"I don't imagine *He* will," Gena said piously, unable to help herself.

His well-defined mouth hardened. "Well, well, Miss Bristle Brush about to take up where Uncle Raff left off. Don't let twenty thousand acres go to your head, honey. You're not inheriting a show-place, far from it. A lot of the run is covered in brigalow, so don't go dreaming up any cosy pictures."

"So why do *you* want it?" she tossed the question at him. "There's got to be some feasible explanation for *your* actions."

He glanced at her briefly. "There is, my avenging angel! Melaleuca is sitting right on my doorstep, covered in wilga. And once the cattle hit the wilga they split up and vanish. It's not properly fenced and some of my cattle are crossing the creeks when they're down and going bush. The whole place is badly in need of rehabilitating. It could be first class, but instead of that huge areas of it are under pear."

"Pear?" She looked at him blankly with visions of ruined orchards.

"Prickly pear," he explained. "A severe menace, but it can be overcome by the *cactoblastis*, a grub that has solved the pear problem in this state. So far as I know it hasn't been put to work on Melaleuca of late. Chad Duffy, *your* manager," he underlined it with heavy emphasis, "is

75

a complete no-hoper, though he found a way around old Raff. I'd run him off my property in double quick time, and I'd advise you to do the same."

"I'll form my own opinions, Mr. Brandt," she said steadily, stung by his tone.

"Sure you will, honey, and you'll suffer for them. But a little suffering might be beneficial in your case. You're just another big headache laid at my doorstep."

She twisted her hands in her lap. "I don't see how you can say that. You don't even know if I'm staying."

Strange lights flared in his eyes. "Oh, but you are, aren't you, Gena? You've got your toes dug in. You're a stubborn little filly."

She had no answer to that, but stared out at the flying miles, the swimming sunwash of wide open country. The jeep slashed along a blue-shadowed track where the musky sweet smell of the bush cajoled the air. Gena felt the blood tingle in her veins. She took a deep breath, filling her lungs with warm, spicy air. The late afternoon sun gilded the glossy tops of the kurrajongs to a canopy of flames and she was struck into silence, her ear attentive to the urgent voices of the birds; thousands of them as they homed in with declining day. The voices were flutey, cackling, deep golden-toned, the plumage so brilliantly varnished as to be startling. On the ground nothing was moving, except sunlight gliding swiftly in and out of the trees. Dense patches of wattle clustered along the water-holes and Gena's inexperienced eye recognised the shade trees of peperina and the red-blossoming bottle brush, and there were waterlilies thrusting their pink buds in the distance where the grass grew long and green.

A soft sensuous sigh rippled up from her throat. The cattle baron acknowledged it with a slight smile.

"Don't be afraid to show your enthusiasm, honey."

Sunlight suffused her face and throat and turned her hair to newly minted gold.

"I can see why your ruling passion is the land," she murmured feelingly.

His voice deepened. "Not at all, Gena. I've more interesting ones!" He turned to look at her and one black eyebrow shot up in devilment. Gena felt boneless, quiescent, her heart pounding with a deep rhythmic beat.

"Well, *I* think it's beautiful," she repeated steadily. "With a beauty and dignity not easily found. I'm just drinking it all in, yet I'm thirsty for more."

He smiled, an easy charming smile. "Careful, honey, you're beginning to unwind, like a skein of silk. The Outback can have that effect on you." His eyes were clear and challenging, wide set under dominant dark brows. His strong mouth was amused.

Gena looked over to the western horizon where the high leaping flames of sunset were shooting into the sky. She was very aware of him now, her arm almost brushing his own. For a moment she yielded to the enchantment of the moment and the scene, while his physical magnetism seeped right through to her bones.

He turned to give her a curious glance and his skin glowed a richer, deeper gold than his eyes. Gena looked back at him speechless, her own eyes wide open and unguarded; time seemed to be meaningless, unimportant, the sensation of belonging quite insane. A stone bounded off the bodywork of the jeep and its loud crack jerked

77

her back to reality.

"It's only a little way off now," Brandt announced off-handedly, and accelerated hard. "Just around the next bend."

All at once Gena was tense and curious too. Her first impression was bad, for a huge sign greeted them, nailed to the double stock gates that sagged wearily on their hinges.

PRIVATE PROPERTY – KEEP OUT
THIS MEANS *YOU*

She looked at him appalled. "Take it down," she begged him.

"Is that an order, ma'am, or sheer recklessness?" There was some slight hardness in his voice that made her look at him.

She swallowed on a lump in her throat.

"It doesn't look friendly!"

He threw back his dark head and laughed with a charm as deep and effortless as his voice.

"Your wish is my command!" He stopped the jeep, pulled on the handbrake and swung on to the ground. Gena, watching him, heaved a sigh of relief when he was back in the vehicle with the offending sign stowed away in the back.

What she could see of the surrounding countryside was good – open ironbark country, thickly grassed – and the impression lasted right up to the homestead.

Melaleuca, named like Bauhinia, for the prettiest woods of the Outback, was a low, rambling bungalow type building and the days of its glory were past. Wide ver-andas surrounded it and the eaves were so low Cyrus

78

Brandt ducked his head instinctively, although a man of his height could just clear them. An old squatter's chair guarded the front door, looking out towards the creek, and bougainvilleas ran a wild crimson riot over the cast-iron railings.

Gena trod on a loose floorboard and it sprang up and hit her a hard knock on the shin. A ferocious frilled lizard, disturbed by their presence, scuttled across her foot and she jumped with a frisson of repulsion, feeling a nervous sweat prick out across her palms.

"Home, sweet home!" she burst out jerkily.

"I expect you're just feeling hungry," the cattle baron murmured, on the brink of laughter.

She coloured a little with resentment. The unconscious arrogance of the man aroused the aggressive spirit in her.

"You're so young, Gena," he drawled. "Why do you colour when I look at you?"

"If you're trying to embarrass me, then you're succeeding," she said in a flat composed voice.

He tipped her chin and walked ahead of her, flinging a few switches. The interior sprang to life. In the living room the furniture was old, but good, basically English styled pieces and loosely grouped to face an enormous brick fireplace wall. The patterned fabric of the upholstery the curtains and the scattered rugs was faded and worn and dismal old portraits marched around the walls.

Gena walked wordlessly into the dining-room where the position was even more dismal. The walls were sheafed in dark walnut, but the sideboard looked a genuine antique. Characteristically she began to rearrange things in her head, seeing herself doing a few landscapes to brighten the sombre-toned furnishings. The rooms were large and airy, but they badly needed the feminine touch. She would have no difficulty there. In fact the whole place represented a challenge.

A last ray of sunshine slanted across the room and Gena stopped in her tracks, incapable of movement or speech. A finger of light caressed the portrait, touched the smiling mouth and the eyes. The pain of loss was intolerable! Tears sprang to her eyes and she rubbed a hand in a childlike gesture across them. The radiant young face continued to smile back at her. Gena, yet not Gena, for the features were rounded, the bone structure less pronounced, but the eyes and the mouth were identical, the heavy gold hair.

It was Virginia, and Gena's heart ached with long buried longing. "Oh, Mummy!" she whispered broken-heartedly, and lowered her face into her hands. Such eager young life to have been so cruelly snuffed out. And *she* was the cause of it – a new-born child!

The man moved swiftly, crossing the room and drawing her into the hard security of his arms.

"It's been a long, emotional day for you, Gena. Just take it easy now."

She rested against him, fighting the wild impulse to weep and weep and weep, and heard him murmur into her hair, "No wonder at all I knew you. I've been looking at that portrait for a long time now. Come now, child, get a few things together and I'll take you back to Bauhinia."

She drew away from him then in deepest consternation. "But I'm staying here. I'm not at all nervous!"

"Well, *I* am!" he said tersely. "I can't leave you here

without even another woman for company. So far as that goes, I know a married couple who would be ideal for the purpose."

"But I'm perfectly all right. I don't need anyone. I'd rather have the house to myself."

He frowned and his strong-featured face took on an even more powerful cast.

"This isn't idle politeness, Gena. Nothing annoys me more than signs of independence in a woman."

Her voice was vaguely conciliatory. "I know the bush is rather eerie after dark, but I'm really not the nervous type. You must believe me."

"The bush!" He looked at her in complete mystification. "What in the loving world are you talking about? Listen here, young lady, I don't know what you're talking about, but I mean just this. You have about seven stockmen working for you and the bunkhouse is only a few hundred yards away. If that's not bothering you it's bothering me. You're not exactly old and ugly."

She looked at him in surprise. "Heavens, you sound like a mother hen!"

His face held a disturbing quality. "I've never been called *that* before."

"Do you mind?"

Strange lights flickered and receded in his eyes. "Take care, honey, my palms are beginning to itch."

"You frighten me!"

"I have done. Very easily, in the past. You're only a babe in the woods for all your brave front!"

She flushed under his satirical gaze. "Such things are best forgotten!"

"I agree!" His dark face had a slightly wicked look. "But we're straying from the point. I can't leave you here alone, surely you can see that?"

Almost on cue there was a knock on the front door and a sandy-haired man, not tall, but very solidly built, walked slowly into the living-room. His greenish eyes were deep set in his head and they darted restlessly from the man to the girl.

"Evening, Mr. Brandt. Evening, miss. Chad Duffy, your uncle's foreman. I just came up to offer my condolences and see that you're settled in all right." His voice was very frank, very sincere, but something about him made Gena uneasy.

"How do you do, Mr. Duffy," she said defensively. "I noticed you at the funeral." Cyrus Brandt said nothing at all and she felt extremely uncomfortable.

The foreman's eyes flickered. "I know you won't want to be bothered now, but I'll be at your disposal to show you around the property and answer any questions you may have, first thing in the morning."

"Thank you, Mr. Duffy," Gena said, her unease increasing. She didn't much care for the way those small green eyes were flicking over her with veiled appraisal.

"Thank you, Duffy," the cattle baron said in flat dismissal. In the face of the bigger man's silent menace Chad Duffy decided on a quick withdrawal.

"I'll say good evening, then, ma'am." He gave Brandt a quick respectful nod. "Evening, Mr. Brandt." As his footsteps receded along the gravelled path the cattle baron burst into violence.

"This is a hell of a set-up! What are your people thinking about?" he asked angrily.

"I do my *own* thinking, Mr. Brandt." Gena's eyes sparkled at his tone. "You're making a mountain out of a molehill. I'm really very self-sufficient, much as you loathe it." She tossed her hair and went to walk through the open door.

She might have guessed at what he would do. But she didn't. He caught her up as she passed him and swung her into his arms. Gena was dumbfounded, unable to forgive him.

"There's a heavy penalty for kidnapping in this country, Mr. Brandt!"

Those curious little flames licked up in his eyes. "Rather that than a fate worse than death, as the saying goes," he drawled maddeningly.

"You're crazy!" She found his blend of cynicism and mockery infinitely disturbing.

"Am I? I've lived a lot longer than you, honey, and I don't trust that Chad Duffy one little bit. He hasn't the intelligence of one of my packhorses. Now do you grab your nightie and a toothbrush or do I?"

"I will," Gena breathed sweetly, showing him a furious face.

He shrugged and lowered her to the floor. "That's the spirit," he said approvingly. "Men rule the world and make all the rules, and all you've got to do is grin and bear it."

It was ridiculous to be affected, but she was. "You're a monster! An ogre! And you take yourself too seriously," she trailed off under his sardonic look.

"I never let sentiment interfere with business, Gena,

and this is business."

Gena almost danced from the room. In the dining-room she shoved a few things into her overnight bag.

"Oh damn, damn, damn! This would happen!"

"Try to bear up under the strain," he followed her up lazily. "You'll be a better girl for it. Now I don't want to hound you, but let's shove off. I've got my best girl waiting."

"Oh yes, I know the language all right!" she said with a touch of heat. She got to her feet and let him lead her out to his jeep. She felt a little giddy. How easily this man was managing her – much against her better judgement. Or was it? On reflection she decided she didn't alto-gether trust Chad Duffy herself.

The red glory of the sunset was at its zenith, but soon a soft purplish haze would invade the sky.

"How far to Bauhinia?" she asked with quiet despera-tion.

"Ten miles by the road, less when the creeks are down. But we can't take the short cuts at the moment. Why don't you close your eyes for a bit? You've lost colour. You whip yourself along far too much."

"Don't forget to add that we're not compatible. That's always a strain." She lay back, doing what she was told. In truth she was exhausted. "How lonely Uncle Raff must have been," she murmured sleepily. "Why did he hate you?"

"Close your eyes," he ordered crisply.

Gena gave up, bemused and out of balance. The jeep bounced over narrow bush tracks while her head kept slipping sideways. "Much more of this and I'll go to sleep on you," she announced.

He grinned. "It might be worth trying, but for the lord's sake don't snore. A snoring woman I just cannot abide!"

"That settles it!" Gena sat up straight. "I hope your best girl doesn't object to visitors."

"I've a feeling she won't object to you, Gena. Now be quiet, you drive me crazy."

"Oh, what a charmer!" She tilted her head and let her thoughts flow on uninterrupted. The evening breeze danced and ruffled the leaves and she surrendered herself to the beauty of the evening; the wild torrent of birdsong.

He was the first to break the silence. "Do you ride?"

"I once had a rocking horse!"

"Do you or don't you?" he repeated patiently. "A simple yes or no will suffice."

"A bit of each!"

"Good God!" he looked at her, his voice vaguely irritated. "I'd better get you fixed up with a quiet little mount. Keera should be able to give you a few lessons. She's a superb horsewoman."

"And that's all?"

His burnished eyes touched her face like a shock of electric current. "God give me patience! You badly need taking in hand."

Gena sank her teeth in her lip. "I'm sorry," she found herself saying. "Sometimes I'm a bit too quick off the mark."

"Sometimes!" His voice conveyed a nice shade of meaning.

Gena looked away from him out of the window. In just under fifteen minutes the great wrought iron gates leading to Bauhinia loomed up, flanked by the countless pink and white blossoming bauhinias that gave the station its name. Cyrus Brandt stopped the jeep as they looked out on the magnificent view. It was a land of tremendous space and silence. On that clear evening they could see over miles of countryside right away to the ranges, dark shapes on the skyline.

Gena gazed her full in a trance of weariness and pleasure. Over in the distance was the property's own sale yard with its grassy sale ring and tiers of white seats, and further on again was the landing strip with a light aircraft standing on it.

"Now I know what you mean by a showplace," she said with a hint of dryness in her voice. "Even at a distance it has an unmistakable atmosphere, a kind of legendary charm."

"Kind words, ma'am," he smiled at her lazily and leant forward to turn on the ignition. Gena sat back, determinded not to show too much enthusiasm. After all, she was a property owner too and her father had designed many beautiful homes. But Bauhinia *was* beautiful, from that very first sighting of its great wrought iron gates. It crested the hill like a Spanish hacienda with the last wash of the sun glancing rosily off its whitewashed walls, the curved symmetry of its rows of arches.

Gena's mouth softened and parted expectantly. She looked about her with curiosity and pleasure. The jeep cruised up the circular drive and came to a halt beside a rock garden of massed succulents and a chattering waterfall. Gena clambered out without assistance and waited for Cyrus Brandt to catch up with her.

Doors of amber glass stood open to them, revealing a generously scaled entrance hall with its tiled floor and brilliant Moorish rug. A stark contemporary landscape by a famous Australian painter decorated one wall, flanked by two magnificent planters holding lush indoor plants. The result was a cool, stylish introduction to the whole house. Through the twin arches that opened off on either side of the entrance hall Gena could see into the living and dining-rooms, where the rough rendered white walls made a perfect foil for dark traditional furniture and dazzling colour accents. She stood there storing away details to pass on to her father.

Within seconds of their arrival a small, wry-looking woman approaching her sixties hurried through to them, pushing back a curly wisp of what had once been her crowning glory. It was obvious that their arrival had been noted. The woman wiped her hands on her crisp white apron.

"You're back, Cy. Just as well. I can't get young Becky settled, much less off to bed. And she's barely had a mouthful to eat." The soft, good-natured mouth quivered as she fingered a cameo brooch at her neck, her only attempt at decoration. "And this young lady is –" she peered shortsightedly at Gena.

"Miss Gena Landon, Cass, Melaleuca's new owner. Mrs. Cassidy, Gena, an indispensable member of our household."

"The housekeeper, miss," Mrs. Cassidy snorted. "To be fair, though, I *am* indispensable." She hesitated, but only for a second. "I was sorry to see your uncle go the way he did, believing things he should never have believed, doing things he would never have done . . . once. They got to him, that's what. Not at all like I'd expected things to be."

"That will do, Cass," Cyrus Brandt said with finality, and put a hand on her shoulder. "Gena will be staying overnight – I didn't care to leave her up at the house by herself."

"I should say not, indeed!" Aggie Cassidy looked disapproving, something she did well.

"I'm not nervous, Mrs. Cassidy," Gena said for the third time that night.

"If you're *not*, then you *ought* to be. You modern young women! I've never seen the like. Not suitable at all. Traipsing all over the countryside by yourselves . . . much too pretty for your own good. Now what about dinner? What would you like? The guest rooms are always aired and made-up – no problem there. You can take your pick."

Cyrus Brandt waved a hand, careless, authoritative. "Thanks, Cass. Anything at all will do for dinner. I'll leave it to you. I've never known you to go wrong yet. Now where's Becky?"

"Out in the playroom. See what you can do with her, though God knows it's her mother's job – and her a thousand miles away drowning her sorrows." Mrs. Cassidy stood there with her shoulders up and her lips pursed. Her hands were tightly rolled in her apron and unhappiness stared unhindered from her face.

"Cass!" The deep voice pulled her up and she obliged reluctantly.

"All right, all right, I'm going." She turned impassive blue eyes on Gena. "Pleased to meet you, young lady. I hope you eat a decent dinner, and don't peck at your food."

"I'm absolutely starving, Mrs. Cassidy," Gena said with simple truth.

"Glad to hear it," the lady retorted, not to be outdone.

Cyrus Brandt laughed. "That's our Cass, and no apologies! She's twenty-four-carat gold. Now, Miss Landon, would you care to meet my favourite girl?"

Gena smiled, a young uncomplicated smile. "That's what I'm here for."

He laughed under his breath and led the way through the house. There was too much of it to take in all at once, but Gena got the impression of elegance and distinction, a continuity of style that flowed from room to room, and above all, the relaxed atmosphere of Outback living. He paused outside a small room off his study and turned the door handle. The room was brightly furnished in yellow and white, papered in nursery themes and lined with toys. In its centre sat a very small girl, perhaps four or five, abandoned in some private dream world. Facing her in a semi-circle sat a gorgeous bevy of dolls, a blonde, two brunettes and one redhead. They could have been on the point of having their hair brushed or a bedtime story being told to them, Gena couldn't tell which, for the little girl looked round and the dolls went toppling in a waxen heap.

She hurled herself at the man like a small creature of the wild; as though life couldn't hold anything sweeter. Cyrus Brandt swung her high in the air, then lowered her, pressing kisses into the tender little nape. The child butted her head into him, locking her arms behind his head, hiding her face, inarticulate.

"And what have you been up to, my little courtesan? Not in bed after all Cassy's efforts? Never mind, it doesn't matter. I've brought someone to meet you. Her name is Gena and I think she looks rather like Doll-Doll."

Becky looked up and for several seconds stared into Gena's face, obviously thinking. Finally she wriggled out of the man's arms and trotted over to where her blonde doll lay in a taffeta heap. She picked it up, patted its dress down and carried it back to Gena, looking up at her intently.

Gina knelt down to the little girl's level. "I'm sure I'm not half as pretty as Doll-Doll. And I haven't got her lovely curly hair. Is Doll-Doll really her name, or is it Joanna?"

The small face didn't change, not by a flicker of expression. But Becky was a beautiful child – a tea-rose! Glossy black curls clustered round her creamy little face dominated by enormous gold-flecked eyes. *Those eyes!* Her frame was tiny, too fragile, and she looked to Gena as though she didn't smile often.

Gena took the soft little hand separating the fingers. Her own hand felt cold, a little clammy to the touch. *The eyes were unmistakable.*

"I don't believe your name is Becky at all. I think it's Rosebud! It suits you." The child continued to stare at her, but she didn't pull away. The quality of her expression was unusual, remote and unattached to the world around her. Gena persisted, "You're a lucky girl to have such lovely dolls, Becky. I see you have a blackboard too

90

and lots of coloured chalks. Can you draw? I can. I can draw lots of things. Koalas and possums and kangaroos, and I can even draw a goanna. I nearly trod on one tonight. It gave me such a fright. I nearly screamed, and that would have frightened your Uncle Cy, because he's a scaredy cat."

The rosebud mouth relaxed, and Becky looked up at the man as though she had tapped some secret well spring of delight. Gena was unbearably touched by that expression of bright pleasure. She got up and walked over to the blackboard. "Shall I draw a goanna?" she asked lightly. "I wonder what colour to use?"

Becky followed her over to the board and began the serious business of selecting a chalk. Finally she passed one across to Gena.

"A *pink* goanna, Becky?"

The black curls bobbed, but Becky remained silent.

"A pink goanna it is." Under Gena's hand a very realistic goanna took form. She didn't stop there, but continued to cover the blackboard, drawing and talking nonsense. Soon the board was covered in engaging bush creatures; creatures that Becky would instantly recognise; koalas and bandicoots, a joey peeking out of its mother's pouch. A fat wombat waddled across the top of the board and four little emus decorated the corners. Becky kept her supplied with chalks and Gena filled in with all the improbable colours. As she reached for the duster Becky lifted one of her blonde plaits and held it, peering into Gena's face. Gena turned to the child, a smile dawning.

"Are you going to tell me you like my drawings?"

Cyrus Brandt moved for the first time. His black velvet voice was even and steady, but disturbing for all that.

"Becky hasn't spoken to anyone for eight months now. But one day soon, she's going to run across the room and say – I love you, Uncle Cy. I can wait for it. It's going to happen. It has to." His voice fell almost flat as though with hopeless repetition.

Over Becky's rigid little head Gena met those strange burnished eyes. They plainly told her to say nothing. She swallowed hard, a little dazed with the shock of it. The events of the day were too confusing. She simply couldn't cope. Gena took Becky's cold little hand and pressed a chalk into it.

"Now it's your turn to do something, Becky. I think we'll draw a cat. They're nice and easy to start with and they do have such lovely whiskers. I saw a tabby cat outside on the drive. Was it yours? Let's draw it." She spoke over her shoulder. "You can go away for a while if you like, Uncle Cy. Becky and I are going to draw a cat before she goes to bed. Aren't we, Becky?"

Becky moved nearer the blackboard, her hand gripping the chalk in readiness. At the door Cyrus Brandt turned. "You're quite a girl, Gena. Just keep it short for both your sakes."

Gena nodded without speaking. Her eyes were stricken with tears; the tears of heightened feeling. Her mind still shied away from the fact that Becky was mute. She felt in a strange state that was almost empty-headed and she had no idea what the next six months would bring. Becky noted her tears, jewel bright. The topaz, black-lashed eyes looked into Gena's, steadily without curiosity. Becky was used to seeing people cry!

CHAPTER V

BY the end of the month Melaleuca homestead was barely recognisable. Gena had never felt so tired and so happy and so over-excited all at the one time. She woke each morning in perfect harmony of body and mind, feeling that the new day would be so much more rewarding than the last. There was so much to be done and in another fortnight Linda and her father were expected to fly out for their first visit to the property. Letters had sped to and fro and according to instructions Linda had freighted out a selection of drapes and slip covers suitable for wielding instant magic on the old home. The effect was more than satisfactory, Gena decided, for the vitality of the contemporary prints lifted the old furnishings out of all recognition. The hardwood flooring and the wall panelling always in fashion gleamed with an ageless lustre, even if it cost Gena a few not-to-be-parted-with pounds in body weight.

That particular morning she planned to turn her attention to the bedrooms. She thought she would strive for an old-world effect. The colonial pieces alone would give her a head start. From the kitchen she heard Mrs. Simmons speaking gently and persuasively to Becky, trying to coax the child into having a glass of milk and a biscuit. Thea and Frank Simmons were now a fixture at Melaleuca whether Gena liked it or not. The cattle baron had seen to that! Fortunately Gena liked them both. They were likeable, hard-working bush folk and they minded their own business. Their bungalow, adjacent to the house and joined to it by a roofed concrete path, was completely self-contained, and Mrs. Simmons took over the cooking for the stockmen as well as helping in the house. Her husband, an expert cattleman, tried his best to work under Chad Duffy, who was *not*, until such time, as Mr. Brandt put it, Miss Landon saw fit to get rid of him. Gena acknowledged to herself the necessity for this, but she was awaiting her opportunity. One just couldn't march right up to the man and say "You're fired!" The moment would present itself. She didn't like Chad Duffy, that was true. It was an instinctive thing, but it had to be admitted that he was working well enough under the new owner. Huge areas of pear were daily being conquered.

Gena carried her array of patterns and textures into the living room, calling to Becky, her sweet and constant little visitor, to come keep her company. Becky came running. A close bond had sprung up between the two, born of Gena's liking for children and her endearing creative ability. There seemed to be nothing Becky liked more than to sit on the floor beside Gena going through her old sketch books and portfolios; the countless illustrations of toddlers and older children; their toys and their pets and all the paraphernalia of childhood. But Becky had never put her pleasure and interest into words. Not once, though Gena had dreamt of a miracle. Looking down at the glossy little head with its short bubble of curls, Gena's eyes pricked, not for the first time. Cyrus Brandt had not been forthcoming with details, but Aggie Cassidy had. Old family retainers would talk and Aggie was no different from any other.

The tragedy began with a motoring trip to Melbourne to see Sir Joshua Hyland, Keera's widowed father. There was some sort of an argument along the way – perhaps the constant bickering and by-play Keera liked to indulge in. Then the smash! According to the hysterically distraught Keera, Becky had flung herself sideways at her father, causing him to lose momentary control of the car. Fate took over. The big high-powered car, travelling at speed, skidded on gravel and plunged into a tree. Gavin Brandt was killed instantly, his wife and child thrown clear – mercifully unharmed, or so it was thought. Since then Becky had never spoken. She had seen all the experts and they were all in agreement. The damage was not physical. The child was in shock. She would speak again when she was ready – no one could say when. That was eight months ago. Keera Brandt, always a temperamental, high-strung woman, seemed unable to cope with her life, her child, her grief, or her guilt. According to Mrs. Cassidy she junketed around all the capitals, leaving the care and responsibility of her child to her dead husband's brother. Her father, Sir Joshua, although devoted to his little granddaughter and shattered by the tragedy, was an old man with a precarious heart condition. Out of all the jumbled information Gena gleaned one fact: the only person Mrs. Cassidy seemed to entirely approve of was Cyrus Brandt, and he shone like a demi-god.

Gena broke out of her reverie. She reached over and patted the little girl's cheek, feeling its exquisite texture. They exchanged a smile and settled down to a companionable silence. Later on in the morning when Mrs.

Simmons brought Gena a welcome cup of coffee Becky consented to drink that glass of milk just to be friendly.

Gena was just cutting out a decorative valance for her bedroom curtains when she heard the jeep pull up in the drive. Her heart began its usual erratic pounding, but she sat there, pretending a cool collection – the lady of the manor, as she put it to herself.

"Anyone home?" His voice always held that thread of mockery. She would know it anywhere, that way it had of conveying so many different shades of meaning. She willed her own voice to sound no more than casually friendly.

"We're in the living-room!" Becky scrambled to her feet eagerly, only to plonk down again. The moment Gena looked round she knew why. Cyrus Brandt was not alone. A woman accompanied him – a woman richly different, as arrogant and casual as a man. The combination of red hair with great glistening dark eyes was so striking that Gena could hardly take her eyes off her.

In exchange Gena was being subjected to an intense and prolonged scrutiny, but strangely enough it was completely without offence.

"You could greet your mother, Becky," the woman said jerkily in a rich husky contralto. Her nostrils flared with some intensely suppressed emotion. The child didn't move and the woman swept on in nervous agitation.

"Don't let's bother with stuffy introductions, they bore me to tears. You're Gena, I know, and I'm Keera – Keera Brandt, Cy's sister-in-law and Becky's mother."

Gena moved towards her and took the long slender hand. "How do you do, Mrs. Brandt," she said very politely. "I'd no idea you'd returned."

"Not an hour ago." Keera Brandt's dark eyes searched blindly around the room. "I flew in with a few friends. They've come up for the sale."

"Wednesday, on Bauhinia," Cyrus Brandt inserted deftly. Gena swung about in time to catch him watching her with the careless, deliberate, indolent way of his that made the blood beat in her cheeks. The topaz eyes gleamed then shifted to Becky. "Don't I rate a kiss, Becky, my lamb?" He held out his hand and the child emerged from under the pile of sketchbooks. She flew across to him, making a wide circuit of her mother.

Keera's mouth was a slash of scarlet in her dark golden face. "Cy tells me you've been very good to Becky. I can see she's happy with you and I'm very grateful. God knows I'm not much use to her." You could try, Gena thought silently, feeling a stirring of latent sympathy for the woman. She seemed on the verge of some sort of breakdown. Aloud she said: "Becky's very interested in my drawings and I love having her with me. I used to be a commercial artist before all this . . ." she swept her arm around the room. "I've done countless children's illustrations in the last two years and it's come in handy. My father sent all my old sketchbooks out to me."

Cyrus Brandt, with Becky in his arms, sank into a recently upholstered chair. "You're altogether a surprising young woman, Gena. You've worked wonders on the house."

His sister-in-law's fine dark eyes swept around impassively as though she could scarcely visualise the "before" picture. Gena almost smiled.

97

"How long do you think you can stand it?" Keera asked tautly. Gena looked genuinely puzzled. "This life," Keera explained herself. "The Outback life. It's a love-hate with me. I tell myself I'll never come back, but I always do. The silence! It's deafening, isn't it? Positively deafening."

Gena studied the handsome, moody face opposite her. "I'm right at the love stage, Mrs. Brandt. I've never felt so well, so happy in my life. The bush is beautiful and the air is like wine. Everything's so splendid and remote I'm going to start painting again shortly, when I've finished all this."

Keera looked at her speculatively, her head on the side. "Perhaps it's the novelty, dear. It may wear off. *I* should know it. *You're* not old enough yet to be obsessed with fears for the future. I've been in an anxiety state since I was about twelve." She smiled without humour. "Don't wait too long, Gena. Even a beautiful girl has to make plans, and you *are* beautiful, aren't you . . ." the scrutiny grew more intense . . . "like a sculpture hammered out of gold," she observed dispassionately.

Gena flushed. "You're very kind."

"Not my words, dear, though they're apt enough. Cy's." Keera turned her head. "Aren't you going to come over to me, Becky? I've brought something beautiful back for you and something from Papa Josh."

Becky went rigid, her small face unnaturally strained. Keera jumped to her feet and circled the room with her hands in the air. Her great eyes were swimming with tears. Gena bit her lip, feeling the woman's pain and inadequacy.

"Don't mind me," Keera jerked out. "I've always been over-emotional. I never thought I'd see the day when that would happen – yet it has. I wish I was dead!"

Her brother-in-law cut her off harshly. "Stop it, Keera. You'll alarm the child. Just take things calmly one day at a time. Everything will come right if you're patient and loving." He stood up and deposited Becky gently on the floor. "A change of subject is badly needed. Would you care to come over this evening, Gena? There should be about six of us and I think you'll enjoy yourself."

Gena gave the older woman time to recover herself. "It's not a sewing party, is it?" she asked lightly.

"No, would that appeal to you more? It's just drinks, dinner and some stimulating conversation."

Keera turned back to them. She had a pronounced pallor, but she seemed otherwise under control. "Do please come," she said huskily. "I'd like to talk to you properly."

Gena smiled and her eyes danced with their points of laughter. "Thank you, Mrs. Brandt. Now could I offer you something . . . a drink, coffee . . .?"

"No, thank you, Gena," the cattle baron cut her off in his usual decisive fashion. "We haven't much time. Keera just wanted to meet you. We'll take Becky back with us too. Say good-bye to Gena, Becky. You'll see her again tomorrow."

Becky moved over to Gena and Gena bent down and kissed her, a habit that had now become a ritual. If Becky was avoiding her mother, she still hungered for a woman's embrace. They all moved out on to the veranda and Keera smiled again briefly. "Until this evening, Gena." Unable to help herself, she swept Becky up into her arms and carried her out to the jeep. Becky neither resisted nor cuddled up to her mother. Cyrus Brandt watched them for a moment, on his face a careful blankness.

"I'll get my foreman to pick you up about seven," he said abruptly.

"I don't think I've actually said yet whether I'm coming or not."

He appeared not to have noticed her. "I can run you back myself whatever time you're ready in the morning. You may like to stay all day, for that matter."

Gena perched on the cast iron railing, winding her arms around a smooth white beam. "As usual, you're oddly neglecting to take any notice of me."

He smiled, very briefly, seemingly abstracted. "Just indicate your agreement by nodding."

Gena nodded and swept back her hair with a deft movement. "I must thank you. I must thank you very much."

His eyes suddenly gleamed. "That's quite all right, Gena. You may be able to do me a turn one day."

"Yes, indeed! No one admires your masterful ways more than I do."

"Deep waters, honey. You're getting in too deep."

Gena looked away over the crimson cascade of bougainvillea. "Now that would be the ultimate imbecility."

"Yes, wouldn't it?" he smiled ironically. "For once we're in agreement."

"Why don't you say something nice to me for a change?" she asked blithely, throwing him a shimmery, coquettish look.

"I think I'll retire while we're still at war. It's a whole lot safer." He moved swiftly and took her hand. Gena lost her precarious balance and fell hard up against him, just as he knew she would. "Never start anything you can't finish, Miss Bristle Brush."

He went down the steps swiftly with his familiar controlled grace, but Gena barely looked at him. She straightened up and waved to Keera and Becky. As the jeep pulled away she gave vent to the final, bitter expletive – "Men!" Once she'd said it she felt a whole lot better!

CHAPTER VI

BAUHINIA was a blaze of lights when Gena arrived. She stood under the hectic blossoming stars for a moment, quietly admiring. It was, she concluded readily enough, a paradise in the wilderness, a secluded oasis of sun and flowers. The big station wagon pulled away and she turned to wave to Dave Wells, Bauhinia's foreman.

In the entrance hall she hesitated for a second, her poise and confidence held together by a slender thread. Tonight she was unaccountably nervous and she caught herself wondering what it was Cyrus Brandt really wanted of her. These past few weeks he had seemed bent on cultivating her friendship; if the curious state of verbal combat that existed between them could be called friendship! Cyrus Brandt was a shrewd, unswerving man of ambition. Everything he did had a motive! And he *did* have a very clear understanding of grace and form and a muted kind of magnificence. She swayed slightly, wondering why she was there.

The cattle baron came out to greet her, much too suave and handsome for her liking. The light slanted over his dark head, the coppery skin.

"Come in, child, don't hover. You look like some long-stemmed blossom in a light wind."

She tilted her blonde head with its double chignon and feathery side curls. "Thank you. I knew I could rely on you for a compliment. However, I'm here!"

"Is this surrender, then?"

"Reconnaissance more likely," she retorted swiftly, arching her delicate black brows.

He laughed and shrugged his powerful shoulders. "In that case follow me." Unexpectedly he took hold of her hand and Gena trembled convulsively. The long fingers stroked her palm and a little mocking light danced in his eyes.

"Nervous, Gena?"

"If I am, I'm too proud to show it." Gena tried to sound casual.

He flickered a glance at her. "A man learns," he commented dryly, his tone neatly poised between mockery and laughter. In the living-room, a small group of people were idly nursing dry Martinis, obviously waiting for their host to rejoin them. Cyrus Brandt made the introductions and Gena found herself absorbed effortlessly into the group. Keera flashed a smile at her, svelte and beautiful in brown and black silk jersey, and Gena noticed at once that she looked startlingly and unaccountably younger.

The other members of the dinner party were Brian and Barbara Lang, brother and sister; both tall, well-shaped and springy, and near neighbours of Bauhinia: Mr. and Mrs. Prentiss, a pleasant middle-aged couple and co-owners of a prosperous Southern cattle stud; and Bob Goddard, a long-standing friend of the family, a man in his late forties, heavy-set, with an ugly attractive face and an easy manner.

Gena found herself drawn into conversation with Brian Lang. He wore his light brown hair neatly brushed back in crisp waves from a pronounced widow's peak and his deep blue eyes were warm and admiring.

"Tell me, what do you think of your inheritance, Miss Landon? I suppose you're already arranging to sell out!"

Gena controlled her surprise. "Well, not exactly. I've only just moved in."

He smiled, his teeth very white and even. "Babs and I have been meaning to call on you, but we've been frightfully tied up lately. Trust Cy to keep you happy!" he sidetracked. "The funny part is, Melaleuca's been on my mind these past few days. Thinking it over, I could probable make you an offer myself. Not a lavish one, of course. The old place is in need of urgent attention, as you know. Still, I'm sure it would sound attractive to you."

Gena pleated a fold of her skirt, trying to sound diplomatic. "I'm not making any decisions right at the moment, Mr. Lang. But when I do—" she let *that* trail in the air where it belonged.

"Oh, do please call me Brian," he urged her. "I'm not trying to rush you, Gena. I'd just like you to know I'll have at least *one* offer. Old Raff and I were the best of friends. In fact I was one of the few people he'd allow to visit him right up until the end."

Gena said what was on her mind. "I didn't see you at the funeral."

"No," he murmured vaguely. "Babs and I were in Brisbane at the time trying to negotiate a very tricky sale. We're used to it. But a girl like you wouldn't want to be burdened with the affairs of a property. It's not as if you could sit back and enjoy it, with fat cheques coming in all the time. And it must be deadly dull for you too." His eyes studied her with frank approval. "Now that I've seen you, I feel like taking back my offer."

His gallantry was interrupted by the sudden appearance of his sister, who drifted up to them, without any obvious sign of pleasure.

"So *you're* the famous Gena Landon," she said conversationally. "Cy has told me *all* about you."

"Dear Cy!" Gena tilted her head tantalisingly. "He's told me *nothing at all* about you."

Barbara's big blue eyes widened with a marked lack of fondness. "I can't believe that," she said flatly, and deposited herself down beside Gena with minimum grace. From the peculiarly feminine glitter in her eyes Gena correctly interpreted the "hands-off-he's-mine" warning, and nearly laughed aloud at the irony of it. "And how are you making out at Melaleuca?" Barbara was querying. "The old place was an awful shambles, as I remember."

You're being pretty damned patronising, Gena thought wryly, but managed the light touch. 'You'll have to refresh your memory one day. I've worked absolute wonders."

Barbara's mouth fell open and closed gently. She stroked the wavy brown hair that fell on to her shoulders. "Do tell me about it. It sounds quite fascinating." Her eyes slid over Gena's ivory and gold perfection; the long lovely dress of crêpe-de-chine with its low ruffled neckline and wrist-length sleeves. "It's quite a job trying to visualise you in jodhpurs," she said with smug complacency.

"That's strange. I haven't the least trouble seeing you," Gena retorted, sweeter still. "Very crisp and efficient, skin glowing, smelling horsey."

Tactfully Barbara's brother tried to fill the awkward hole in the conversation. "Tell me, Gena, what did you *do* in the city?" He looked at her with every appearance of interest.

"Not much," Gena smiled back at him, holding his slightly bemused eyes.

"Fancy, you look like you'd have quite a story to tell," Barbara said tightly, her temper showing.

"Perhaps we should call the conversation off," Gena suggested tentatively, controlling a wild impulse to laugh.

Brian Lang patiently tried again. He offered to refill Gena's glass while Barbara turned to wave vivaciously at the cattle baron.

"Cy – poor darling! Do come and talk to me."

Gena's eyes positively glittered with malice. Poor darling! Who would have thought it? She never would herself. Her own gaze became locked with the cattle baron's and she looked away, her mouth twitching.

"Excuse me," Barbara murmured ungraciously, and hurried off to meet her host half way.

Gena felt a certain sympathy with Brian Lang's efforts to appear pleasant and casual in the presence of such pretty, feminine backbiting. "Extraordinarily handsome devil, isn't he?" he observed, evidently not expecting an answer.

Gena had none to offer. The fact was self-evident, and she was reminded of Tony's remark about Lucifer.

"No need to tell you Babs is struck on him," Brian Lang confided. "Something may come of it. We'd like to hope so."

"Indeed?" Gena felt duty bound to contribute something to the conversation. "It would seem rather a lot to ask."

Her companion gave her a slightly baffled look. "I beg your pardon, Gena, I'm not with you."

"Of course not!" Gena brushed her own comment aside. "I'm just being facetious – a bad habit of mine." She let her luminous eyes dwell on him. "Now do tell me about your life as a cattleman. I've often thought it must be the most rewarding career there is," she lied. There seemed no harm in leading him on, she thought impishly. Not with Barbara's hand lingering on the cattle baron's arm, her silky brown head near his shoulder.

Brian Lang beamed on her. Flushed and flattered, he proceeded to do as she asked, hitching his chair a shade closer. "I don't know whether you realise this, Gena . . ."

Gena relaxed with a charming, faint air of helplessness. The feminine suggestion that she couldn't quite cope with the weightier problems without a man's help – Brian Lang found this extraordinarily appealing.

The dinner bell brought his long monologue to a close and Gena wished and found herself rescued by her host.

"You'll excuse us, Brian," Cyrus Brandt murmured smoothly. "We can't have you monopolising our golden faun the entire evening." He leant over and took Gena's hand, drawing her to her feet in one graceful movement. He seemed amused and perversely Gena resented it.

Brian Lang nodded. "I know what you mean. I must say Gena's beauty knocked me sideways for the first few minutes."

"Strange, her brand of chatter usually has that effect on me," Cyrus Brandt remarked glibly.

Gena stirred, suddenly restless, and the cattle baron swept her aside. When she looked back Brian Lang had subsided silently into a cloud of smoke.

"You appeared to be in pleasantly trance-like state, Gena," Cyrus Brandt murmured, his voice shimmering with amusement. "Was the conversation too much for you?"

"That would be dignifying it beyond its deserts," she said tartly, without giving enough thought to how it would sound.

He glanced down at her classic profile. "You have got a sharp tongue, haven't you, honey? You'll have to watch it or you'll go to a lonely spinster's grave."

"The thought doesn't make me anxious," she retorted quite hotly.

"Said without a great deal of conviction but a good deal of heat," he laughed down at her, the iridescent light back in his eyes.

"Oh, you . . . you . . . you!" Gena whispered on an in-rush of breath.

"No one else will do," he capped her neatly with a serene disregard for her efforts to break away from him. "What's up, Gena?" he smiled. "Don't you like me?"

"Ask me something easy," she said huskily.

He acknowledged her slight confusion with a smile. "I can't, my child. I've exhausted my supply of nonsense on Barbara."

The words surged up without volition. "I didn't see you making any effort to break away."

"Things sometimes get a little complicated when you're dealing with a woman." He glanced at her and his eyes were deliberately insinuating. "Why, are you jealous?"

"No," she said swiftly, coolly contemptuous.

He laughed softly. "How you do score!"

At dinner Gena sat between Keera and Bob Goddard. It was immediately apparent to Gena he was also deeply in love with her and at no pains to hide it. Looking into his dark, rugged face and listening to his amusing conversation, Gena decided she liked him very much. There was warmth and humour there, as well as the more forceful qualities that had made him a successful business man.

Bob Goddard was *not* on the land. He bought and sold it on the grand scale from the security of his own statewide real estate business. His knowledge of cattle, however, was formidable. As the talk grew round to the coming sale he had quite a few worthwhile comments to contribute. Bauhinia was one of the first Queensland cattle stations to import pure-bred Brahman cattle from the U.S.A. and its present herd made the stud renowned throughout Australia with a show record unequalled in the Brahman breed. Gena sat listening, as the talk grew more and more involved. Jack Prentiss had the floor with his methods of controlled cross-breeding and boosts to production, and after a while Gena began to get completely bogged down. She had not a smattering of anyone else's knowledge.

Barbara appeared to be an authority in her own right and even Keera offered some fairly knowledgeable comments.

Cyrus Brandt, looking down the table, caught Gena's

wide-eyed look of incomprehension. The sight appeared to amuse him, for immediately he switched the conversation to contemporary Australian art and what was going on in the art world. Gena shone on a subject she found well nigh impossible to hide her interest in. Cyrus Brandt, Keera, and Bob Goddard, all of them collectors, taxed her knowledge to the utmost and it was Barbara's turn to have the conversation fly over her head. She retired wrapped in a silent fury.

The dinner, chosen, supervised and finally seasoned by Keera, was superb, and afterwards the men wandered off for brandy in the study and to continue their high-powered discussion on management stresses, seasonal fluctuations and so forth.

"With men it's business, business, business!" Barbara commented bitterly.

Keera's sidelong glance was full of black-eyed merriment. "You're joking, darling!" she remarked not so obscurely. Gena had to smile. Keera, for all her lush beauty and sophistication, was passionately fond of fine food, its cooking and presentation, and the women found themselves swapping their culinary masterpieces. Very soon Keera bore Mrs. Prentiss off to write down a recipe she professed herself unable to memorise.

Barbara moved nearer Gena on the sofa, crossing her long slender legs.

"Exotic, isn't she? Keera, I mean. The hair's not for real, I remember a time when it was coal black."

Gena was surprised and showed it. "Well, it's a beautiful job. I had no idea it wasn't natural." She held Barbara's mildly accusing gaze. "You don't approve?"

"I wouldn't care to tamper with Mother Nature myself," Barbara murmured repressively, and patted her wavy brown hair.

"Goodness, I thought that was what we were all doing," Gena said lightly.

Barbara looked startled. "Why, isn't yours natural either?"

Gena laughed. "I'm sorry, we seem to be tuned in the wrong wavelength."

Barbara chose to ignore her. "I wonder how long she'll stay this time. It's an awful shame about the child."

Gena, at this point, had the option of suffering a violent reaction or trying to remain calm. She decided on the least antagonising line. "Becky is an exquisite child," she said deliberately, "but she's suffered a severe shock to her nervous system. She's a sensitive, highly strung little creature, but she'll respond in time."

"Well, I for one certainly hope so. I mean, just how long does Keera expect Cy to look after the child? It's simply not fair to the man. Of course, there was a whole lot of talk about them at one time. Not that I believed a word of it, mind you." The angry glitter in Barbara's blue eyes gave her words the lie.

"Well, I for one don't want to hear about it," Gena said sharply, having listened to a great deal in the past.

Barbara contorted her long slim body, trying to see if the others were coming back into the room. "Well, why should you indeed?" she queried briskly. "It has nothing whatever to do with *you*. But for me it's different." Her eyes held Gena's as she launched into a frontal attack. "Brian tells me he's made you a tentative offer."

Gena resisted the impulse to say something frivolous. Perhaps she really would go to a spinster grave. Barbara certainly should, she thought tartly. Aloud she murmured pleasantly, entering into the spirit of things,

"Melaleuca, you mean, Barbara?"

Barbara nodded vigorously. "What else? Of course I'd want to see it first. Father did leave me a quarter share in his estate. I must have my say."

"I quite appreciate that," Gena said gently, her tone implying anything at all. "It just so happens that I have no plans whatever for selling, not at the moment. Beyond this point I'm committed to absolute secrecy."

Barbara looked at her as if she doubted her gravity, but Gena's face was quite bland.

"Surely you realise you can't keep the property on?" she remarked querulously. "Why, you don't even know what a Droughtmaster is."

Gena took a stab at it. "My own cattle are pure British stock," she said crisply.

Barbara blinked. "You're smarter than I gave you credit for. But you needn't sound so damned patronising. You have no idea of the advantages of a Brahman-British cross."

Spare me! Gena thought, but kept her face level.

"Why, they thrive on country where British cattle die." Barbara warmed to her theme, but Gena had already gone beyond her. She came back to earth to hear Barbara say: "Anyway, I'll drive over to your place one morning next week if I have time."

"Oh, do! Come for morning tea," Gena suggested brightly.

"Thanks, I will," Barbara agreed, looking mollified. Both girls looked up to see Keera and Mrs. Prentiss enter the room followed by the menfolk. The evening picked up considerably. Later on there was a big fuss over whether Barbara should be allowed another brandy or not, and in the end it was well after midnight before the household retired. Gena was just brushing her hair, preparatory to bed, when there was a knock on her door.

It was Keera, glass in hand, in the most gorgeous housecoat Gena had ever seen. She was smiling, a little unhappily. "Do you mind terribly if I told you a sad story, Gena? Pithy but pertinent to the situation."

"You go right ahead." Gena moved aside and put her hairbrush down on the dressing-table.

"Bless your little heart!" Keera murmured half in amusement, and wandered into the room. "I'm restless. God help me, I'm restless." They both knew what Keera was going to talk about. She fortified herself in a yellow silk upholstered armchair and craned her neck to see herself in the mirror.

"That's a pleasant surprise! I always expect to look worse. Like I feel," she commented lightly. Gena watched her tip her wrist and drain the glass. "It quenches the thirst and lightens the load," Keera murmured laconically.

Gena smiled. "I'm pretty circumspect with it myself. I find I get belligerent after the second."

Keera laughed. "That's because you're a nice girl, Gena, and that in this day and age is quite an accomplishment. Alas! not mine."

"You make me sound dull." Gena sank into a chair opposite her.

"Don't be silly, dear. I'm old enough to be your mother." Keera twisted her glass idly.

"A very precocious mother!"

"To be sure. But then I was precocious. Not like you, pure and fine like a candle flame. My dear father ruined me with his love and his money and his endless indulgence and my poor mother had no say at all. Yet she loved both of us in her fashion." Keera suddenly looked wan, all her sparkle missing. "The many faces of love," she said feelingly. "There ought to be another name for it."

"No, I don't think so. I like it." Gena gave the matter her full attention.

"Ah well!" Keera smiled tolerantly, then came abruptly to the point. "I'm doing the wrong thing with Becky, aren't I? I can't find the simple, infallible method of reaching my own child."

In the face of such a difficult situation Gena didn't feel she was qualified to offer advice. "I can see that you, like Becky, are still in shock," she said slowly.

The tears started to Keera's eyes. "That's the kindest way it's ever been put, Gena. No, I've failed my little cherub. I turned away from her when she desperately needed me, and I'll never be forgiven for that. I was like a madwoman when it all happened. I really felt I would lose my mind. I had these terrible heads, when everything just used to go round and round and nothing would ease them. I could never have survived without Cy. He's been a tower of strength. I've leaned on him shamefully."

"Well, that's what a strong man's for," Gena said soothingly.

"We were engaged once, you know – oh, years ago, though it never worked out. You can't imagine what Cy was like in those days – the explosive vitality of the man, the life and the laughter. He's quietened, but he's still the same underneath. All force, but he doesn't need to make a show of it. It's there for everyone to see. I love and admire him, but I'm not *in* love with him any more. I gave up knocking my head against that particular brick wall." Her dark eyes misted over with reflection and Gena didn't interrupt her. "I had my chance once, you know, but life moves on. It can never be the same again no matter how much it may appear so on the surface. Why, once I even dreamed of a perfect, pure-bred little lion cub and I would have had a son like that with Cy for the father. Instead I married Gavin, and I have my little Rebecca."

"The brothers weren't alike, then." Gena's voice spilled into the silence.

Keera roused herself. "Oh, very much so, to look at, although Gavin was always a milk-and-water version of Cy, but their natures were very different. Becky is like her father. Shy, introspective, she tends to retreat behind the high walls of reserve. Gavin was like that. I married him out of pique, you know, and I paid for it dearly and so did my poor Gavin. Yet he loved me. We had our moments."

It was very quiet in the room and Keera gave a deep, heartfelt sigh. "I daresay Cy will marry one of these days. There would be a stampede whenever he crooked his little

115

finger." A frown gathered between her brows. "Bob wants me to marry him. We're two of a kind and I'm very fond of him, but I doubt my own ability to make him happy. Then there's Becky. I couldn't present her with one more change. She turns to Cy now for everything and all the time my heart's aching for her to turn to me . . . her mother. Some mother!" she mocked herself bitterly.

"Please don't upset yourself, Keera," Gena said, looking straight ahead.

Keera's face immediately went white. "But I do all the time. I walk about breathing the sad odour of bitterness and regrets. My whole life seems shadowy, insubstantial as a dream. The hopelessness, the barren loneliness of it is driving me to hysteria. It's hard for me to remember my whole world has gone."

Gena jumped up and circled the room, her hands raised in agitation. "Now how can you say that when you have so much? You've no right to despair. Other women cope bravely in the face of tragedy, surely you can manage. You have so much! Looks, money, position, a fine man who loves you, and most of all you have Becky . . . a beautiful child."

Keera lifted her head from her hands and looked into Gena's young, troubled eyes filled with compassion.

"What am I to do? Tell me. I'm listening."

"Just be around. Be here, with Becky. Give her time to love you all over again. All you need is time and a selfless devotion."

"Do *you* really believe it, Gena?"

"Of course I do." Gena's voice shook. She wasn't in

complete control of herself, but she desperately wanted to offer reassurance. "We can all gain something from our mistakes if we're lucky."

"Oh, I hope so, Gena. I hope so." Keera's dark eyes were freighted with doubts. She shook her head slowly, then she began to cry – the hopeless kind of crying, slow and silent and so, so sad!

Gena found the situation overwhelming. Her primary loyalty was to Becky, little abandoned Becky, yet Keera was showing her wounds!

CHAPTER VII

IF Gena imagined a cattle sale would be an exclusively masculine affair that Wednesday on Bauhinia was an eye-opener. The scene looked more like a garden party at Government House with marquees on the lawn and smartly dressed men and women strolling idly over the grounds, heads down, deep in conversation. As Keera explained to her, the social side of the big stud sales was rapidly becoming as competitive as the cattle prices and most of the big stations could be relied upon to turn on a pretty impressive "do". Gena could only agree, if Bauhinia's "do" was anything to go by.

A score of light aircraft stood on the strip, a number from interstate and all of them representing the cream of the big pastoralist families and syndicates. This was the fifth sale on Bauhinia and together with the previous one of Santa Gertrudis cattle was expected to bring in well over a quarter of a million dollars.

Morning and afternoon teas were served in the marquees and a light luncheon provided, but the highlight of the social scene was expected to be the giant barbecue after the sale. Most of the visitors had come to buy, some to study prices, but all of them were intensely interested in the proceedings. At any point on the extensive homestead grounds, one could expect to hear a fairly spirited debate concerning the respective merits of the Santa Gertrudis versus the Brahman.

Gena found herself in company with Brian Lang, looking over the cattle about to be sold. She knew nothing at all about the finer points of breeding, but Brian had undertaken to give her a little elementary instruction. Used as she was to the more conventional breeds of cattle, Gena found the appearance of the Brahmans fascinating. Their kidney-shaped hump, the most distinctive feature, was strong and erect, tapering in thickness and located squarely over the shoulders. Her draughtsman's eye took in all the salient features. The ears were unnaturally long and pendulous; the muzzle full and broad and the eyes, showing the Zebue strain, were slanted and hooded by the loose hide that surrounded them. A few minutes' careful study and Gena felt she could faithfully draw any one of them. The colour of the hides varied from light to dark red and from light to steel grey. Gena consoled herself with the thought that at least the young bulls were being sold into a life of luxury on other stud farms.

Brian walked beside her, pointing out the standards of selection and commenting on the superior quality of the beasts up for sale. He held out his hand and a steer came at a straight walk towards them.

"Very curious, aren't they?" Gena observed, backing a little.

"Yes. They're inquisitive by nature and we've come to believe superior in intelligence. In fact, if they're well bred and handled right, they're easier to handle than any other breed." He paused to give the steer an affectionate slap. "If they're unfairly treated, that's another story. Cattle are only as wild as the man who handles them. The big advantage of Brahmans is their adaptability to tropical conditions; their high level of heat tolerance. You wouldn't take the time to count them, Gena, but the Brahman has sixty per cent more hairs to the square inch of hide than the Jersey. They don't need much pasture fencing either because they prefer to stay on familiar ground. Even the bulls stay with the herd, and that's saying something!"

They paused in front of a magnificent Buddha weighing well over two thousand pounds. The bull stood there motionless on the hot, still day, brooding in his majesty.

"No wonder the Brahman religion made a god of him. He's descended from the Indian Zebu, of course, the oldest existing domestic cattle in the world."

A small boy hurried past them talking twenty to the dozen. "But can you *eat* it, Mum?"

His mother turned to him, faintly irritable. "What, dear?"

"The hump!"

Gena smiled at this snatched piece of conversation and turned back to Brian. "Well, can you?"

"Yes, of course. It's perfectly edible. There's no bone in it. I believe it makes a delicious pot-roast, though I've never tasted it myself." He took hold of Gena's arm and led her over to the show females. "Beautiful, aren't they? They exhibit all the characteristics of refinement and femininity our hawk-eyed buyers will be looking for. There they are over there!" He gestured to the silver gleaming rails of the sales ring, festooned with coloured bunting, where Cyrus Brandt was being photographed with three members of a big Southern syndicate.

The morning passed in a haze of heat, pounding hooves

and excitement, and by lunch-time even the raucous voice of the auctioneer had almost given out. Prices had sky-rocketed by the thousands of dollars, and once, when Gena went to brush a grain of dust from her nose, Brian had stopped her with a vehement whisper: "For God's sake don't do *that*, or you'll finish up with a Comanche Queen!"

Gena sat very still after that. Most of the women present knew all the finer points of breeding and eventually Gena felt emboldened to contribute a little remark of her own about a certain cow's straight walk.

Brian looked his admiration. "That's the style, Gena. It's up to our womenfolk to show an interest. Good cattle mean good quality cheap meat for the table. Why, I've seen housewives in the States pay a small fortune for steaks our women wouldn't even look at."

Gena looked suitably impressed and all in all spent a very educational morning.

Keera and Bob Goddard rescued her for lunch and the three of them dined in the big marquee. There was no sign of the cattle baron, if indeed he found the time for lunch. Professional caterers handled everything from the linen to the glassware and the home-cured hams for the salads disappeared at a tremendous rate. Because of the heat a bar was operating and lean, bronzed individuals in broad-brimmed hats and rolled-up shirt-sleeves quaffed innumerable ice-cold beers without turning a hair or raising their voices.

Barbara and Brian had commandeered a couple of long tables for their crowd and Brian twisted to wave a friendly hand. Gena gave him a quick smile of non-encouragement while Barbara pretended not to notice the exchange. She was otherwise occupied in competing for the maximum attention from the young men of her group. It was obvious from their uniform expressions that Barbara was not quite so popular with her girl-friends.

Several people holding cups of tea paused to offer Gena sympathy and to pass a charitable remark or two about her uncle, but on the whole an air of gaiety pervaded the atmosphere. Everyone was talking with great animation about everything in the wide world *but* cattle, and Gena guessed correctly that they were making the most of the Outback's infrequent social gatherings.

The afternoon was a little quieter than the morning and when Barbara learned that Gena was anything but proficient on a horse nothing would do but that they should make up a riding party. Ordinarily Gena would not have responded to such a blatant invitation to make a fool of herself, but the day's activity and an unaccustomed glass of wine with her lunch lent her a false sense of confidence in her own ability.

Barbara seemed pleased with her decision. "I'll fix it for a few of us," she promised brightly. "Cy has any amount of horses available, but there's a parade of the Arabs, so we can't use *them*."

The news was no disappointment to Gena. A plodder would do equally well. Finally five turned up at the stables. Gena, Barbara and Brian and an engaged couple of Barbara's acquaintance. Gena's horse was called Midnight. She admired its beautiful coat, of necessity, ebony, but most of all its docile demeanour. She stroked its velvet muzzle and tried to make friends with it and happily Midnight nudged her for more.

A few feet away Brian was remonstrating with his sister.

"Couldn't you have found her a quieter mount if she's not done much riding?"

Barbara frowned; she was the more forceful of the two. "Allow me to know my own business, Brian," she said loftily. "In any case the only nag quieter just so happens to be lame today." *That* was a downright lie, but Brian never saw fit to check up on her. So Midnight it had to be.

Gena sauntered over to the mare, trying to resurrect a piece of advice she had read somewhere. *Bridle and stirrup leathers!* That was it! Bless her photographic memory. *Check the tack.* She proceeded to do just that, hoping she looked blasé about it. She walked round to the other side and checked the girth strap. Barbara and the others had already mounted in one synchronised glide. They seemed to be regarding her in slight puzzlement.

"Need any help to mount?" Barbara asked sour-sweet.

Gena understood her only too well. For answer she put her foot in the stirrup iron and swung herself into the saddle far more vigorously than she intended. The mare acted up, then miraculously quietened.

They were off, with Gena and Brian bringing up the rear. Midnight was responding well and Gena began to enjoy herself; the unfamiliar sensation of being in a saddle again. Barbara had already worked out their route. They cut through the citrus orchards far away from the crowd and circled out into the open country overhung with shade trees.

Sunlight dappled the ground where cattle were resting, heads down, mute and incurious. From some distance came the voice of a stockman singing, expending a great deal of energy. They came down at a steady walk on the bridle path that led to the Pink Lagoon. The grass was waist deep in parts and sprinkled with tiny white daisies. The narrow sheet of water glittered like green glass anchored with the beautiful waterlilies that gave it its name. The heat lay heavy on higher ground, but down in that breathless glade it was deliciously cool. Gena relaxed, feeling sensuously abandoned to that beautiful place. She would come back by herself some time and sketch those lilies, pushing out their tightly closed buds. A composition began to form in her head. Linda had space on her bedroom wall for just such a painting. There was a hypnotic spell about the place after the busy murmur of the grasslands and it brought a new expression to her face.

Brian found his eyes straying continually to it. Her hair seemed always to be caught in a shaft of dusky sunlight and it glistened greeny-gold. A loud warbling broke out above them in the bauhinias as a blackbird began his tireless rhapsody. Barbara rode up ahead, quietly meditating, and Gena had to admit that she was a splendid horsewoman. She sat her horse beautifully relaxed yet with firm control over it; her every wish transmitted along the reins.

Brian's eyes swept rather shyly over Gena. "You're doing very well there!" His remark must have wafted on the wind to his sister, for immediately Barbara broke out into a fast canter. The canter gave way to a gallop. Gena gave Midnight a little rein, but the mare didn't need pressing. It flew after the others, its instant response throwing Gena's body off balance.

She tried to regain mastery, but Midnight couldn't be stopped. Spent blossom dropped on to her head and she realised Brian was shouting to her, but she was totally committed to staying on her horse. There wasn't even time to panic, for the pace was terrific. Then suddenly Midnight stopped abruptly and Gena went hurtling over his head, only then conscious of blind panic. The thickly grassed shelf broke her fall. She lay spreadeagled, dazed and winded, her face colourless and contorted until blessed air rushed into her agonised lungs. The trees made a green whirlpool around her, reaching for her and drawing her into their leafy arms.

"Gena, Gena!" She came out of that pit of senselessness to see Brian looking into her face, waiting for her to speak. Barbara, ashen-faced, was behind him with her two friends feebly making clucking noises of sympathy.

"I hope to God no bones have been broken!" Brian was muttering with increasing pessimism.

Barbara pushed him aside and ran strong hands over Gena's bruised limbs. "Don't try to move for a moment," she said grimly.

"Don't worry, I can't." To Gena's surprise her voice came out at no more than a croak. She lay there for minutes on end while they all stared back at her with varying degrees of anxiety. Gradually the world swung back on its axis and the sickening, spinning sensation passed.

"You should never have put the mare to the gallop if you couldn't handle her." Barbara's voice grew accusing, the more so because she couldn't shake off a feeling of guilt.

Her brother cut her off very smartly for him. "Turn it up, Babs, not *now*." He looked down at Gena and his voice was gentle. "Do you think you can stand up, Gena?"

"That's the fifty-dollar question! However, I'd better try. It's very undignified the way I am."

The two men helped her to her feet, holding her until her legs felt ready to take her weight.

"I'd better get Cy." Brian appeared to come to a decision.

"There's no need to do that," Gena said more hysterically than she realised. "Pride comes before a fall. I don't want everyone to know about it."

Barbara looked at her with a glimmering of admiration. "Do you think you can ride in? It's not that far."

"We'll take it slowly. In stages," Brian added, softening the blow.

Gena had no other recourse than to attempt it. Brian was exquisitely gentle with her and they all remounted and followed in procession back to the homeground. Gena and Brian came in last. Outside the stables he helped her off her horse as though she was eggshell china. The sun fell over her like a waterfall and Gena almost groaned at its brilliance.

Brian was talking to her and Gena had the feeling that he had been saying the same thing over and over again. The name "Cy" impinged on her consciousness. Then he was there, towering over her and staring grimly into her paper-white face.

"What in God's name have you done to her?"

126

Even Brian wilted and fell back at the force of his tone.

"I'm most dreadfully sorry, Cy. We were out riding and Gena had this damned awful spill. I wouldn't have had it happen for the world!"

"Spill!" the word split the air. "She can't even *ride*. Surely you had the nous to see that?"

Brian tried ineffectually to defend himself, looking more like a schoolboy than a grown man.

"Actually, Cy, she was doing quite well."

The cattle baron looked increasingly dangerous.

"Oh, leave it, there's a good chap. You go on, I'll attend to her."

Brian backed away with further muttered apologies, but the cattle baron cut him off. "You might tell Barbara I'll be having a word with her."

Brian paled and hurried off in search of his sister.

They were alone. He held her shoulders, trying to see into the still white oval of her face.

"Gena, look at me, you crazy little fool. Do you place no value at all on your life and limbs?"

But Gena was only on the fringe of things. "Such tenderness," she murmured almost incoherently. "You'd make a wonderful lover!" She collapsed against him and he smothered a violent oath and swept her up into his powerful arms.

"There's one thing certain — if you stick around, you'll sure as hell find out!"

She tried to look at him. "Cyrus, the Persian king!" she said faintly. Her head lolled on its flower-like neck, then she fainted, crumpling up against him like a small

127

frightened child.

Keera proved to be a very good nurse, calm and re-sourceful. She even swept aside all thoughts of the bar-becue to look after Gena. She held the girl's throbbing head when she was violently ill, sponged her wan face and helped her into a gorgeous ice-blue nightdress two sizes too big for her.

An hour later the doctor had been and gone and Keera judged it time to run a deep hot bath for Gena to soothe away her aches and pains. Gena protested modestly, but Keera kept the bathroom door ajar, just in case her pa-tient felt faint and happened to slip under the water.

She took up a position just outside the door with a wide-eyed Becky listening to Gena's humorous account of the afternoon's ride. When Gena came to Barbara's part in it Keera could contain herself no longer.

"The bitch! She's beyond redemption!" she exploded in violent sympathy. "How perfectly horrible!"

It was then that Becky smiled at her mother. Keera, witnessing the miracle, crushed down her natural desire to smother the little flower face in kisses. She merely smiled back at her little daughter and took Becky's hand. Becky didn't pull away at all!

By seven o'clock Gena had a tray in the guest-room and by eight o'clock when Cyrus Brandt looked in on her, she was already fast asleep, one silver-gilt pigtail over her bare shoulder, a profusion of cushions supporting her aching limbs.

CHAPTER VIII

MELALEUCA shone with cleanliness and order by eight-thirty the following Saturday morning. The oak floors gleamed and fresh flowers from Bauhinia's gardens stood at strategic positions proclaiming a welcome. When Chad Duffy presented himself at the house to outline the routine for the day he found his employer looking exceptionally stylish, with a town make-up and a country gilded skin. The flush of excitement stood out on her cheekbones. Everyone on the station knew her people were expected out for the week-end.

The foreman's greenish eyes slipped over her covertly and his voice became as insinuating as treacle. The new Boss-lady was very fetching to the eye and much too pretty to live by herself. Gena scarcely noticed him, her mind a closed circuit filled only with visions of her father and Linda. The last look, however, really got through to her and she dismissed him in a very businesslike fashion.

Chad Duffy walked down the stairs slowly. He took a last drag at his cigarette and ground it out under his foot, taking his time about it. When the Boss-lady got mad her eyes shimmered like the lake! He liked a woman to show a little spirit and she couldn't be a prude. Not a girl with those looks!

Inside the house Gena vaguely realised she would have to take decisive action. And soon! It was a pity. She disliked unpleasantness, but Chad Duffy would have to go.

129

There was nothing else for it. The kitchen door opened and Mrs. Simmons came in bearing a cup of coffee.

"Time for a hot drink," she said in her friendly tone. "You've worked like a slave, my dear. The place is a credit to you."

Gena sat down, shrugging off the problem of Chad Duffy.

"And to *you*, Mrs. Simmons," she pointed out fairly. "I couldn't possibly have gone right through the house without your help. Now come and join me. All we have to do now is sit back and relax. They should be here very soon."

Thea Simmons smiled and went off to pour herself out a "cuppa". She didn't share Gena's penchant for coffee.

By ten-thirty Paul and Linda still hadn't arrived and Gena walked aimlessly through the house, straightening cushions, unable to settle to anything. Surely nothing had gone wrong when all their plans had been so carefully made. They were to fly to Rockhampton by a national airline, then pick up the small charter flight to land on Bauhinia's strip. Cyrus Brandt had teed it all up with the charter company and he had even offered to drive the new arrivals over to Melaleuca himself. Surely nothing *could* have gone wrong!

The long minutes passed and just as Gena began to get fretful she heard the sound of a car horn coming up the drive. Pleasure and relief flooded her whole being. She glanced into the mirror for a last-minute check on her appearance, then flew out on to the veranda, unable to control her smiles. It was quite extraordinary how much she had missed them both, though she never fully realised it

130

until that very minute!

Bauhinia's big bronze station wagon swept up the drive and pebbles splayed out from under its heavy tyres. Gena ran down into the sun, shielding her eyes from its imperious splendour. The big car slid to a halt under the shade of an ancient wattle and Cyrus Brandt got out. He smiled at Gena lazily, his eyes noting every detail of her appearance.

"Your family, present and delivered, ma'am!" He walked around to hold the door as Linda and Paul Landon emerged from the other side. Gena went to rush forward to greet them and was halted in her tracks.

"Gena, my duck!"

She spun, breathless, unable to credit her eyesight. It was Tony, wreathed in smiles! Clearly he had mistaken her precipitous rush, for he covered the intervening space in double quick time, grasping Gena to him and kissing her roundly.

"Tony, what a surprise!" she said quite truthfully. It only took a few more seconds for her to recover her aplomb.

"There, I knew you'd be pleased!" Tony beamed at her in a world of his own. "I'm *not* mistaken, am I? It was the greatest good fortune I rang your father."

Gena was spared the necessity for answering this. Linda made a rush at her, looking exceptionally pretty and ... yes ... confident, and that much plumper too! The two women embraced with warmth and affection and Linda breathed into her ear, her blue eyes impish with humour, "We will speak in whispers – later!"

Gena smiled and transferred herself to her father's

131

waiting arms. She laid her blonde head against his chest as she had done since she was a child.

"How wonderful to see you, Dad!"

"And how I've missed you, chick. We both have. Tony too, I do believe," he added dryly.

Tony, not a foot away, was still beaming on everyone, including the cattle baron, who was looking suavely sardonic.

Gena turned to him with a charming show of neighbourliness.

"You'll be able to stay on for a while, won't you, Cy?"

The cattle baron's eyes gleamed at this overwhelming display. Gena had never been known to call him "Cy", even once.

"I'd like to, *Gena*," he drawled deliberately, "but I have the vet coming this afternoon." He turned to include the whole party in his devastating smile. "However, I'm looking forward to having you all up to Bauhinia tomorrow evening."

Linda took Gena's arm, blushing prettily. She seemed in no way abashed, however. "Mr. Brandt has very kindly invited us to dinner. We told him how you were in raptures about his house. Your father was very interested in all your detailed sketches."

Gena coloured hotly and the cattle baron laughed. "She never told *me*," he murmured significantly.

"Oh well, perhaps that's the more complimentary way of doing it." Paul Landon looked amused and extended his hand to the younger man. "Thanks once again for all your kindness. Linda and I appreciate it. And Tony too, of course," he added as a polite afterthought.

132

Tony rallied, his smile increasing in scope. He *was* acting very much part of the family, Gena thought, half amused, half annoyed with him. One would have thought he was the man of the moment!

They all stood back to wave the cattle baron off and fifteen minutes later Linda seized the opportunity to tell Gena her great news. Gena collapsed into the nearest chair.

"But surely you know for sure?"

Linda bloomed like a rose. "If I were ten years younger I'd be supremely confident. But at my age . . .!"

"Which is no age at all . . ."

". . . I can't believe in my good fortune."

Gena simply melted. "If you're right and you know darn well you are, it's absolutely super. Father will be beside himself with happiness."

"You don't *mind*?" Linda looked up to ask helplessly.

"Oh, don't be so perfectly asinine! *Mind!*" Gena said scornfully, and got up to drop a kiss on her stepmother's head. "It will make life quite perfect."

That really did it! The ready emotional tears sprang to Linda's blue eyes and rolled down her cheeks. The tears of sheer happiness more than anything else. She smiled mistily through them and leapt to her feet, rushing out of the room to repair the damage.

Gena stood for a minute singing a snatch of a song to herself. Through the open windows she could see out on to the veranda. Tony was holding her father in a spirited conversation. Her father turned and saw her and smiled happily. Gena understood at once what that smile meant, just as her father guessed at the meaning of her own. It was all Gena could do to refrain from handing him a cigar there and then!

It turned out to be a long beautiful day full of laughter and contentment and just enough movement to prepare them for the next delicious meal. Gena found she derived a considerable amount of pleasure from Tony's company. As none of them could claim much skill on a horse Paul Landon used the old Ford to drive them around the property.

Gena's first impression was that Chad Duffy had been busy. The sheds and stockmen's quarters had benefited from a fresh coat of paint and they looked neat and well kept for the visitors' inspection. They doubled back past the back of the homestead where a windmill was clanking over a flourishing vegetable garden. Further down, Frank Simmons was busy pruning the citrus trees and he took time off to wave to them.

New double gates replaced the old ones that had sagged so wearily on their hinges and great stretches of the boundary fence on Bauhinia's side had been repaired. The Ford took the well-defined tracks that led through the open iron bark country to the main watering places and the mustering camps with their yards, a dip, and a small horse paddock. The cattle, with a few exceptions, were good Herefords with livered hides, white faces, white bellies and touches of white on the flanks. They stood in good pasture country feeding back to the scrub.

On the outskirts of the brigalow scrub they stopped to look out over the silver grey sea. The undergrowth was crisscrossed with logs and fallen branches, dense with wilga, the savage lawyer vines and the insidious prickly pear. Only that week Chad Duffy had sent four men out to poison the scrub – a next to hopeless task, for it grew back twice as relentless.

Back in the car again they followed the line of the creek, watching the drovers bring in the young bullocks for yarding up.

"The peace, the absolute peace!" Paul Landon turned to smile at them. He tooted the horn and the drovers waved their wide-brimmed hats. "You've quite an inheritance, chick!" Almost at the same moment Tony was whispering to Gena in the back:

"God, it's rather empty and isolated, isn't it?"

She smiled at the conflicting opinions. Despite his views, Tony exclaimed eagerly at every kangaroo, emu and goanna that crossed their path. The sun gilded the long green spear grass that stood up on the ridges and an emu stepped out from behind a bank of it. Always curious, it decided to pace the car to look in at the occupants. It raced madly down the bank and alongside the car, turning on a terrific burst of speed. Its long legs shot up and down like piston rods and its ridiculous tail feathers flopped madly. It levelled alongside, then craned its long neck to look in at them.

They were still laughing when they reached the turkey scrub, the home of the wallaby and the bush turkey and almost inpenetrable. The sun was coming down over the ranges when they turned back towards the homestead, but they had seen a surprising amount of the property for one afternoon.

Paul and Linda went in to rest before dinner while Tony and Gena sat out on the lawn. Tony seemed more amused than anything else with Gena's inheritance.

"It should bring you in a few threepenny bits, love," he commented sagely. "It never hurt a girl to have a nice little bit of dowry."

Gena smiled, "Who said anything about selling?"

He looked his surprise. "Don't tell me you're not going to. You'll have to, dear girl. Call off this bushwhacking bit and step back into civilisation. Have done, as it were!" He lay back on the grass staring up at her. "I've never stopped thinking about you, Gena. You know that." He screwed up his eyes thoughtfully. "I don't much like the idea of the cattle baron across the way."

Gena raised her delicate brows. "May I ask why?"

Tony shrugged, equally delicate. "Well, I ask you. Middle-class morality and all that. I mean, a woman's not safe!"

"Perfectly safe, I assure you."

Tony sat up abruptly. "Well, there's no need to add a silent 'worse luck!' That even penetrated my thick skull."

Gena gave him a wicked sidelong look. "You don't seem happy!"

Tony fell back again on the springy grass. "You bet! I'm feeling very uncheerful, very letdownish. Here I am, a fine upstanding sturdy lad, killing himself for love of you."

"Don't dramatise yourself, dear. You'll get over it," she said unfeelingly.

He sniffed. "Perhaps you're right. One doesn't like pity from a woman." He sat up again and made a grab for her. "Come here, my slim golden creature!" He held her hard with her head under his chin. "Let's post the banns.

Think what a lot of fun it will be. You'll never be lonely again." He tilted her head to gaze into her wide, luminous eyes. "Presumably you're occupied by thought, dear girl?"

Gena was, seeing in her mind's eye a dark profile, clear-cut like a medallion. The physical memory came back to haunt her like a dream. Tony shook her slightly, his thin face aware and searching.

"So the lady looks beyond me!" The soft warm air brushed in scented waves over them. "And that's the difference between loving and not loving," he said with deepest irony.

She blinked rapidly. "I'm sorry, Tony."

"I'm sorry, too," he said grimly. "And there's no need to look at me as though I'm the headless ghost on the blasted heath. Let's go in, my golden-haired child, I've had nothing to eat all day bar the occasional meal."

Morning brought some unexpected visitors in the guise of the Langs – brother and sister. They apologised profusely when they realised Gena had visitors, but accepted Gena's invitation to come in and meet them. Barbara, at her best in male company, positively sparkled. She looked very tanned and healthy in beautifully cut jodhpurs with a cream silk shirt, her blue eyes gleaming. It was, Gena decided, the garb that suited her best.

After a few polite preliminaries Linda excused herself to make morning tea. She was never one to linger, besides, she remembered something Gena had told her once in a letter about a certain Barbara Lang. Gena looked over to where Barbara was making an all-out effort to captivate Tony, who was acting out the part of a shy young man.

Brian Lang pulled his chair closer to Gena's father and began to outline the natural advantages of Melaleuca, adding at length his idea of how best to go about the job of rehabilitating the property. Paul Landon sat listening idly and nodding his head from time to time. They were quite pleasant young people if a little obvious in their intentions, but for the short time remaining to him he preferred to have his wife and daughter's exclusive company. He interrupted Brian briefly to urge Tony to accept Barbara's charmingly issued invitation to see over Langlands the following day.

Tony, left without rearguard action, was forced to accept with feigned pleasure. Tony was a one hundred per cent follower of the bright lights and Barbara's offer left him cold and forlorn.

It took Linda little under fifteen minutes to produce a delicious and lavish morning tea. It took less than half that time for it to disappear, but it was close on midday before the Langs judged they had made their interest in Melaleuca sufficiently clear.

Everyone walked out to the veranda in the buoyancy of parting and Brian took Gena's elbow and led her down to the station wagon.

"Look here, Gena, now that I've spoken to your father I'm sure he'll urge you to sell out. Quite apart from anything else he must worry about you, so far from home," he said considerately. "Babs and I had a good look at the property on the way over. We came the long way round to take in some of the mustering camps. There's more good country than I thought on the run. Babs is nearly as keen as I am."

138

Gena yielded to temptation. "How nice!" she said sweetly.

Brian smiled back at her with a marked lack of perception. "By the way, I noticed that chap Simmons. Works for you, does he? He's always been Brandt's man. Pretty high-handed chap too. Came right out and asked me what I was doing there. I said I was visiting."

"Well, that's all in order, then," Gena returned noncommittally.

Brian continued to smile down into her upturned face. "I must say you've worked wonders with the house. I barely recognise it from old Raff's day. The woman's touch!" he pointed out agreeably. "Babs and I were so worried about you after your spill. Cy really took to us, I can tell you. A bit unfair, though. No after-effects, I hope?"

"Not so it shows!" Gena answered quite calmly. "Well, I won't hold you up, Brian. It will be quite soon time before I come to a decision regarding the property. But I'll remember your offer. What is it, by the way?" she suddenly swung on him.

Brian retreated a step. "Now, now, don't let's talk business here and now. When you're ready to sell out, let me know, and I'll come up with a fair price. Babs and I could improve the herd no end. All a cattle man lives for is to improve his herd," he informed her earnestly.

"It sounds wonderful," Gena murmured, earning herself another admiring glance.

Behind them Barbara was busy making last-minute arrangements with Tony. She raised her voice a fraction. "You'll come too, of course, Gena." Meeting the very blue gaze, Gena got the message.

"Thank you, Barbara, no. I couldn't leave Father and Linda."

Paul Landon, standing up on the veranda, smiled at his daughter's light satirical tone. Between the two of them they had engineered a few blissful hours on the morrow. They were bound to be tired anyway after a late night at Bauhinia. He was mildly surprised to find how much he was looking forward to it. Cyrus Brandt had impressed him enormously and Gena's letters, covered in little pen sketches of this and that architectural detail, had intrigued him and aroused his professional interest.

Linda moved over to rest against his arm and he shifted it to encircle her slightly fuller figure.

"Roly-poly!" he whispered affectionately into her ear. From the way Linda smiled and blushed no two words could have sounded nicer.

Down by the old acacia, Tony wasn't nearly so cheerful. He waved the visitors off with regulation warmth, waited until the station wagon turned the bend in the drive, then said miserably: "Phew, that's enough of that little lot! I almost feel like throwing in the sponge."

"Now, now, it isn't *that* bad!" Gena tried to console him. "You must admit she's pretty!" *That* didn't even raise a smile.

"Pretty!" Tony almost shrieked. "You know darn well the hearty outdoor type brings me out in a rash."

"Then why in heaven's name did you accept?"

Tony made an odd gesture of irritation. "Common courtesy, I suppose. What else?"

"My poor Tony!" Gena took his arm gently. "Do come

in and I'll open a bottle of something for lunch."

"I should think so too. Keeping one's guests supplied with liquor is the first law of hospitality." Tony hardened his arm around her, to which pressure Gena deliberately denied a response. It was no good. She had far too much on her plate already.

Tony glanced down at her sun-touched profile. "It's quite commonplace for a young man to fall in love and equally commonplace for him to be rejected, but come what may, I'll always be fond of you."

They both laughed and walked into the house, tranquillity restored.

CHAPTER IX

DINNER at Bauhinia was effortless perfection. No guest could have wished for a more charming or attentive host . . . or hostess . . . and Keera was unquestionably that. She looked striking in an exotic caftan, as stylized as an orchid, her manner so warm and relaxed, even Linda thawed out under such benign graciousness.

The food was superb, the wines excellent, and the conversation skimmed the surface of things, social and sparkling. Gena found herself laughing a great deal, crushing down the certain knowledge that it was the cattle baron who had buoyed up her existence until the very landscape looked different. She kept her eyes away from him most of the time, feeling without looking the power that moved out to her, creating deep waves of feeling. She had known the moment they arrived that it would be a good evening and she was grateful that her father and Linda would have such pleasant memories to carry back with them to Brisbane.

Bob Goddard, with a week of his stay remaining, made up the odd number, but he was a particularly amusing companion. After dinner when Cyrus Brandt took his guests off on a tour of the house he remained behind to keep Gena company. Keera turned to give them a little wave, a lovely flush on her dark golden skin. She slipped her arm back into her brother-in-law's with an amusing comment on her lips.

142

Gena turned to surprise a torn, sad look on her companion's face.

"I wonder does it ever die?" he asked, all pretence dropped.

Gena looked down at her hands, for the first time that evening touching truth. "I suppose a little of the magic of first love must remain. The remembered dream ... rapture for some ..."

"Yes!" he answered so quietly that she scarcely heard him. "Yet Cy has an air of belonging to no one," he reflected in the few seconds' pause. "Try as I may I can only see him as the better man. He's acted extraordinarily well in a difficult situation, and little Becky adores him." He turned to Gena, his dark eyes clear and steady. "I guess you know I love Keera. I make no secret of it. I want to marry her, some time very soon. Look after her and young Becky. It's all I've ever really wanted, I think. I can't remember a time when it hasn't been Keera, though I've known a lot of women. Keera's been quite a playgirl too in her time, but all that's over. She's got to settle down, take up her responsibilities. She tells me Cy is part of her girlhood – Gavin too, of course. Poor old Gavin! But he was always an extension of Cy. She never fooled me for an instant. I used to feel so sorry for Gavin there at times. They were temperamentally unsuited, I always thought."

Gena looked away carefully. "Keera told me the two brothers were very much alike ... to look at." -

"Yes!" His glance was piercingly shrewd and alert. "To look at, and Becky is her father all over again. *Gavin.* He was a softer, blurred edition of Cy. And that's one

143

reason Becky loves her uncle so much: his strong resemblance to her father. Of course Cy's marvellous with her as well."

If I'm not careful I shall cheer aloud, Gena thought. So Becky looked like her father – *Gavin.*

"I do hope all the experts are right," she said, her voice betraying her release of tension.

"So do I, my dear. Not only for dear little Becky but for Keera as well. You wouldn't know it to look at her tonight, but she's not far from breaking point. Even loving her the way I do I can't pretend she's handled the situation well. But then she's led too self-centred an existence – too much love and attention. You can't imagine the way she was brought up. Old Josh treated her like a little princess, denied her nothing – not the best upbringing for a naturally autocratic temperament." He laughed, but humourlessly. "No self-respecting man would chase after a woman like I've done. The strange part is I'm supposed to be a shrewd business man, with a reputation for ... ah well, when it comes to Keera ... I'm an also-ran. And she badly needs a strong man."

"Don't we all?" Gena said.

His sidelong glance was discerning. "You'll get one, young lady. It stands out a mile. Now here I am bothering you with my problems when I should be asking you how you're making out at Melaleuca."

Gena smiled. "Just fine. I love it. You must come over with Keera and Becky one day. I think I have the house under control."

"But the run's a different story," he said shrewdly. "I'm not interfering in any way, but if you decide to sell

144

I'll handle it for you, as a personal favour, which means no commission, my dear. I'm very grateful for your nice way with Becky and Keera too, for that matter. She speaks very highly of you." Gena flushed, but he didn't appear to notice. "Cy hasn't approached you, has he? I suppose he might get round to it. He's been after that property for a long time. Nearly had it too at one stage. Then the whole deal went cold on him. Old Raff was to have the house and an acre of ground for his lifetime. It was the land Cy needed to spread out."

Gena raised her eyes. They looked sombre. "Everyone seems so certain I'll sell out. *Why*, do you suppose?"

His smile was understanding. "You have to be realistic, my dear. There are some spheres where a woman can excel, but not running a cattle station. That's a job for a man. You could have a good manager, of course, but there's always got to be the man to keep his eye on things."

"Yes, I suppose so," Gena said with a tinge of hopelessness in her voice. "I've just been coasting along, enjoying myself. I suppose I'll have to come back to reality pretty soon." She found it easier to be completely frank with him. "I can't sell to Cy in any case, not unless I want to lose the place."

Bob Goddard whistled beneath his breath. "So things got as bad as that! Old Raff turned on Cy with a vengeance, didn't he? No one seems to know why. You couldn't get a straighter man in business than Cy. I should know, I've handled enough of it. Everything's got to be legal and above board."

"Well, be that as it may, he's out, with me. It's stipulated in the will. The property would be sold up. I'd get a share and the rest would be divided equally between three charities."

There was surprise and bewilderment in her companion's eyes.

"You haven't told Cy?"

"No, and I don't intend to."

"He hasn't mentioned the subject?"

"No."

"The plot thickens!" He looked at her with a quizzical grin. "I take it this is in confidence?"

"Yes," Gena nodded her head.

"And it will remain so," he said quietly. "I'm surprised and unhappy to hear it, all the same."

"Brian Lang has approached me. He seems very interested."

"Oh, take no notice of him," he bit off the words rather scornfully. "He'll want you to give it away, then make you feel he's doing *you* a favour."

Gena smiled wryly, more to herself than him. "It seems my inheritance could develop into a dilemma."

He reached over and patted her arm. "Never that, my dear. You'll have any number of offers and if you allow me to handle it for you, a very good price. Enjoy yourself while you can, but remember what I told you for the future." He half closed his eyes. "If Keera would only marry me I'd buy it off you myself and you could name your own price. If that ever happens . . ." he trailed off a little unhappily. "We could spend six months in the city and six months on the property. I've always had a mind to be a cattleman. I've made all the money I want."

"Lucky you," Gena smiled.

"Money won't buy love, my dear. Like they say in the song." He checked as Tony ambled back into the room smiling warmly. He addressed the older man with raffish charm.

"I bring a summons. Mrs. Brandt respectfully requests your support to back up a crumbling argument."

Bob Goddard got to his feet with alacrity. "In that case, I'd better go. I have no other alternative."

Tony sank down in the vacated chair. "Charming situation, isn't it?" he said chattily. "Eyes less acute than mine would say *he* was in love with *her* and *she* is in love with *you know who*!"

Gena gave him a long cool look. "Whom, surely? But how strange you should gain that impression."

Tony's face sharpened. "You made a horrible mess of that, didn't you, darling? Your eyes are so wonderfully transparent. They always give you away."

"How awful! What do they do?" Gena asked with every appearance of interest.

Tony chose to ignore her. "Don't kid yourself, kid," he started out on his own track. "You're only an incident in a long eventful chain. I've seen the cattle baron looking at you, eyes sliding over that lovely skin coming out of that little black dress."

"You're mad. Quite mad!" Gena said witheringly.

"Far from it, my poor girl. Yes, the cattle baron has noticed how nicely shaped you are, the damnably handsome fiend!"

"The only way to stop you is a flat change of subject. I've just read the most interesting article on Jack Brabham, thrice racing car champion of the world." She clasped her hands hopefully and looked into his face.

Tony responded. "I'm all ears," he drawled laconically. "It's rare to meet a young woman who can converse with any degree of fluency on the subject."

The evening continued in an aura of warmth and pleasant grouping, and Keera took Linda along with her to just "peep in at Becky". Linda was quite genuinely enchanted and the quick tears sprang to her eyes as she remembered the sad contents of one of Gena's letters. Keera herself said nothing, but the two women exchanged a look of deep understanding.

Alone for a moment, Gena drifted out on to the blue-shadowed court, turning her face up to the star-studded night. The wind had lowered, carrying the scent of oleander and jasmine.

"A Bacchante greets the night!"

She turned at the sound of his black velvet voice. He held a bottle of champagne and two beautiful long-stemmed glasses in his hand. She smiled at him with sweet enchantment.

"You've gauged my mood nicely."

"A man would do almost anything for a smile like that." He put the glasses down on the table and turned to fill them. Gena walked into the golden circle of light. She accepted her sparkling wine, her heavy lashes veiling her eyes.

"*Salut!*" he said, his eyes lazily admiring. "I like you in black, Gena. It's very ... becoming. And I like your young man," he added, his voice quivering. "He has a very acute mind. *And* a remarkable eye for detail."

"He's not my young man," Gena informed him between sips of wine.

"Forgive me," the cattle baron bowed. "I must have misconstrued a light flirtation for something of deeper rapport."

She tried to return his easy mockery.

"Without a doubt. For your interest, I have designs on no man!"

"What a pity!" His eyes gleamed and his dark face looked saturnine. "One more?" he asked, taking her empty glass.

She nodded her gleaming head, gratefully accepting. There was no point at all in trying to get the better of the cattle baron, though she just had to try it!

"I thought perhaps we might see Barbara tonight," she said in a light friendly tone.

He gave a low laugh. "I've no prepared answer to that piece of feminine logic."

"Well, really!" she shrugged delicately. "I thought you admired her with great ardour and respect."

He regarded her out of half shut eyes, the corners of his mouth twitching. "Vanquished before I've begun! You've over-coloured your picture. But I'd be happy if *you'd* regard me as your friend." He looked at her with complete self-assurance, his voice alarmingly gentle.

"Heaven preserve me from my friends!" she taunted him deliberately, "though I like you well enough."

"Thank you. Cold comfort, but better than none." His brilliant gaze rested on her face and bare shoulders. "Now, let's just enjoy the light of the moon, shall we?"

She turned her silver-gilt head to offer an apology. "I'm sorry," she murmured contritely, "I have no manners."

One black eyebrow went up. "And why do you think I'm being so excessively forbearing?" He loomed behind her, elegant, satirical.

A star fell and Gena looked out on it, seemingly absorbed in the spectacle. She turned back only to find him a hair's breath away. There was total silence – the silence of glass that could shatter at any minute. Iridescent insects fluttered past them. The lamp lent a magical glow to Gena's hair and she shivered in her low-cut gown.

"Queen and huntress, chaste and fair!" he murmured narcotically in her ear. Gena visibly trembled like a reed in the wind. "The moon!" he pointed out dryly.

She dared not turn towards him. She was stubborn and proud and she dared not give him the upper hand. It was no easy thing for a doe to gambol with a cougar. Suddenly everything seemed too much for her – the moon, flowers, music, the relentless murmur of the cicadas, the man at her side. The melancholy in her beautiful eyes deepened.

"All you need to be an angel is a harp!" he taunted her with incomprehensible mockery. "Won't you turn to me, Gena?"

"You may well ask," she said unsteadily, her eyes shimmering like crystals of ice.

"What's so very terrible?" His hands closed on her bare shoulders to turn her round to him. He looked very tall, cool and calculating with his back to the light. "Why are you so shaky?" he continued conversationally.

Gena couldn't find her voice. Not a sound could she

force through her parted lips. She felt utterly paralysed, knowing one false move could bring utter chaos.

Tony, following them out on to the terrace, saw them and came on undeterred. "I say, what are *we* doing out in the garden?"

"I give you three guesses," the cattle baron said.

Gena flushed rosily at this frivolous answer. She almost flew towards Tony. He gave her a very old-fashioned look, his voice dropping a few decibels.

"Sorry to break up your little idyll, love."

Gena left both men standing as she swept swiftly and haughtily into the house.

On the drive home Tony was abstracted and not his usual extroverted self. Linda, on the other hand, was prettily flushed and voluble.

"What a wonderful evening, and what a marvellous man!" she enthused. "I was quite overcome."

"Lindy dear," Paul Landon interrupted her affectionately, "if you say one more word I shall turn pea green."

His wife gave a low gurgle. "I'd like that, very much. But isn't Keera a striking-looking woman?" she continued, warming to the subject. "I think they'd make a wonderful couple. So rich and handsome and assured. Lovely!" she gurgled.

Gena's heart sank, not for the first time that night. She was haunted by flaring visions of Cyrus and the young Keera, perfectly matched.

"Yes, they seem perfectly matched!" Linda spoke her stepdaughter's thoughts aloud.

Her husband cut her off gently. "Do you think so?"

She turned to him in surprise. "Why, don't *you*, dear?"

Paul Landon frowned, taking the question very seriously. "Well, to be honest, I don't. It's obvious that there's a strong bond of affection between them. But for a wife . . .!" He narrowed his eyes. "I'd say Keera would lose out to someone with the insurmountable advantage of youth . . . and innocence!"

Tony suddenly stirred. He gave Gena a tap on her unprepared cheek. "Nice work, kid," he muttered gruffly.

"Well, thanks!" Gena retorted, coming up with the only answer that occurred to her.

"Next time you hear from me I'll be on the Trans-Siberian Railways!" he remarked astonishingly.

Gena turned to look at him with anxious eyes. "You should have had a cup of coffee. It keeps you awake!"

Tony groaned and kept his eyes closed all the way home.

CHAPTER X

A BIG yellow moon had risen, casting eerie shadows on the lawn. Gena leaned against the cast-iron railing, her eyes trying to pierce the gloom. There had been a power failure, of course, but how had it affected the Simmons? Thea Simmons was always very punctual, very conscientious about her duties. She said she would be home by dark and it was now well after seven! The day had been hot and bright and Gena, after a long foray into the bush, felt tired enough to sleep through a hurricane. But not before the Simmons got home. Perhaps the old utility had broken down! Her deliberations were interrupted by the sudden appearance of a man. She made a great effort to keep her dismay out of her face. It was Chad Duffy.

" 'Evening, Miss Landon!" His eyes flicked over her, appraising her, sizing her up. "I just came up to see if you were making out all right. The power failure not bothering you? A cattle truck ran into a power pole, about ten miles out of town."

Gena stood looking down at him, knowing a sharp sense of urgency and unease.

"So that's it! I was wondering. I hope no one was hurt."

"That I couldn't say." His green gaze whipped past her to the house. "All fixed up with lamps, I see. Know how to use them?"

"Yes, thank you," Gena murmured repressively. She gestured back to the glowing house. "I'm quite all right, as you can see."

153

"I do indeed!" Something very disturbing, very insolent, crept into his voice. He came up the veranda steps, his hair slickered down, his green eyes glowing with a brightness no amount of liquor could dim.

"I expect the Simmons will be here shortly," Gena said, making her meaning quite plain.

"I wouldn't count on it, lady. They're having a bit of trouble clearing the road. Besides, there's no harm in a little company, is there? I mean, it's not a capital crime or anything, is it?" He bore down on her relentlessly, then shouldered past her into the house.

Gena followed him up, aghast. "Mr. Duffy, I dislike to be unpleasant, but I would very much like you to go. You're forgetting yourself."

He swung on her, his raw-boned face unpleasant.

"Pretty contemptuous aren't you, little lady? A sight different when the big feller's around."

Points of ice stood in her eyes. "I beg your pardon!"

He shot her a leering glance. "Oh, don't try that one on me. Brandt, ma'am, as if you didn't know. He sure gets around. Even the old boy was struck on him at one time. But we sure fixed that!" He clamped down on himself as if he had already said too much.

Gena spoke through tightly clenched teeth. "I don't know what you're talking about, but I want you to leave. Right now." This was a detestable, ugly situation, and she felt like a poor, helpless fool.

Duffy was grinning at her and making no attempt to move.

"Not until I've got what I came for, little lady."

Gena quelled a sudden tremor in her hands. "Mr.

154

Duffy," she said tonelessly, "if you don't go away I shall scream and scream."

"Go right ahead. What you need is a man. Now why don't you let me show you how much of a man I can be?"

Fury and frustration exploded in her head. "Get out!" She was shouting now, losing a grip on her control. "Get out, I said. You must be mad!"

He unwound and moved slowly towards her. "We *are* throwing our weight around, aren't we, Boss-lady? But I'm getting a little tired of playing games. You women are adept at them."

A flash of panic struck Gena dumb. His long arm snaked out, closing over her arm, his fingers like talons. "It'd be a lot nicer if you'd co-operate."

She almost spat at him. "Get your great ugly hands off me, you repulsive brute! You're fired!" Even as she spoke she knew it sounded ludicrous, but there was nothing vaguely funny about Duffy's eyes. They were regarding her with a cold and ugly desire, devoid of all sense, all scruple.

"You don't mean that, little lady," he said thickly, and lunged for her, locking her against his heavily muscled chest. "I always make use of my chances, and we're wasting time."

Gena's panic became overlaid with fury. She kicked out viciously, liking the sound of his grunt of pain. The clamped circle grew even tighter and she strained backwards, desperately trying to evade the indignity of contact. She loathed and despised him; she was sickened by the peculiarly scented lotion he had smeared on his hair.

Her throat was parched; her heart pounding loudly. It

155

was only a nightmare. It couldn't really be happening. If she shook herself vigorously she would immediately awaken. Duffy's coarsely grained skin grazed her throat, jolting her back to brutal reality. If she had to she would sink her teeth in him.

"What in hell goes on here?"

The harsh alien voice shocked them into immobility. Then Duffy moved, his shoulders crouched as he flung Gena away from him. She fell hard up against the sideboard, her mind in a tumult.

Cyrus Brandt towered in the doorway, incredibly menacing, his dark face graven in bronze. She had seen him mocking, charming, indolent and laughing, but she had never seen him in a white-hot fury. The sight frightened her. It was frightening Duffy! He looked directly into the strange topaz eyes with their burnish of gold.

"Now don't go misunderstanding nothin'," he started out to say, but the words died on him. What happened next took place in ten seconds of pure panic. Through blurred vision Gena saw Duffy weaving and ducking. She saw his face raked with something more than physical fear. A sickly, insinuating grin curled on his lips.

"It wasn't as if the little lady wasn't willing enough!"

Brandt moved so fast the other man never saw the blow coming. His open hand crashed across the side of Duffy's face, splitting his lip and sending him reeling back against the wall, under the impact of the terrible blow. There was no smile on Duffy's lips now, only a searing shock. Brandt bore down on him and the second blow toppled Duffy over on to the carpet. He folded like an empty sack. Blood oozed from his lacerated mouth and an ugly purple swelling grew under his eye. He rolled with the pain of it, groaning.

"Get up!" Brandt said tonelessly, his very lack of intonation accentuating the impression of imminent violence. He hadn't once glanced at Gena, a slim golden figure crushed up against the sideboard. She moved across to him, her face taut, her long hair dishevelled. She was almost too frightened to touch his arm. He looked a stranger, a complete stranger – raw, elemental man, his strange eyes on fire.

"Please don't hit him again," she breathed jerkily. "He's had enough. Besides, he's bleeding all over the carpet."

Brandt spun his head for a second. "Keep out of this, Gena." The fury was still in his eyes, all-consuming.

Duffy lay still but completely conscious. Brandt swooped and jerked him to his feet.

"That's for the lady. I'll give you *my* reaction if you're not off the property in ten minutes. Take a horse. I don't care if you ride all night, but get going. Your gear will be sent into town."

The blood flushed right out of Duffy's face. It whitened with hate and impotent rage. He got to his feet slowly, shaking his head. Blood gushed from his open cuts and his eye was discolouring rapidly. A seething hate rose in his throat, choking him, obliterating everything else. They were standing close together, ranged against him, Brandt and that so cold little lady. He could wait, if he was patient, awaited his opportunity. He would have his revenge!

Cyrus Brandt followed him out into the night, whistling up Bodalla, his big, pure bred Alsatian. The dog leapt from the jeep and came at a run up on to the veranda. Its ears were pricked, its intelligent eyes gleaming. The man gave it an order, pointing to Gena. The dog settled on its haunches, its splendid head alert, giving the impression it would bound up at any given moment.

Brandt turned back to her, keeping a visible rein on his temper. "Bodalla will look after you until I get back."

Gena's spirits were returning with the colour under her skin.

"I'm all grown up now," she said shakily. "I won't get lonely."

His flashing look of scorn silenced all further comment. She turned and walked back into the house, pushing her tumbled hair back from her face. She went into the dining-room and pulled out Uncle Raff's brandy, pouring herself out what she imagined was a "short snort". Her hands shook and she tossed the brandy off, gagging a little at its fiery aftertaste. She felt ill, a nervous wreck, and so desperately grateful to the cattle baron, though wild horses wouldn't drag the admission from her. After a minute her trembling subsided and she walked back on to the veranda, letting the air blow against her flushed cheeks. Bodalla turned his wonderful head and she spoke to him gently, glad of his company.

Ten minutes later Brandt came back and sent the Alsatian back on to the jeep. It obeyed instantly. He turned to Gena and the look of scorn had changed to one of dark fury. It shimmered off her moon-silvered face.

"Well, he's gone. Months after his time!" He took the steps three at a time. "Tell me, you obstinate little idiot, didn't I warn you about that lecherous swine? What was he doing here in the first place? Surely you had the gumption to get rid of him straight away?"

Gena took a deep steadying breath. "What are *you* getting so outraged about?" she tried to speak calmly, but she was losing the battle. "*I* was the one who was attacked. Though God knows *you* hit him hard enough. You nearly knocked him senseless."

He halted in his tracks, towering above her. "What's with you anyway, you hysterical little idiot? Did you *want* to be raped?"

A strangled gasp escaped her. She swung up a hand as if to hit him, then thought better of it.

"What a vile thing to say to me!" she reverted to a whisper. Her eyes burned with tears of fright and fury so close to the surface that another word from him would send them hurtling down. The effect of the brandy was too invidious. "There are more good women in the world than there are men worthy of them!" she said with trembling conviction.

"Yes, and have you noticed how dim-witted they are!" His face changed, lost its frightening aspect. "I'm sorry, Gena. Virtuous young women are something of a rarity in my bawdy existence." His tone picked up, perceptibly hardened. "And Duffy's too, judging by the way he was acting up. Don't you know when you're playing with fire? Hasn't life taught you anything at all?"

Gena's tenuous control was flaring out of bounds.

"How dare you misjudge me?" she stormed at him. "How *dare* you!"

"Misjudge you!" Twin points of rage stood in his

159

eyes. "Listen, you sweet little moron, can you imagine the effect it had on me coming in here to see you grappling with that dreg of humanity? It's a wonder I didn't *kill* him."

"Oh, shut up!" she cried hoarsely, breathing with difficulty. "I refuse to go with this Machiavellian inquiry. So there!"

"Why, you little vixen! I've a good mind to ..." A frown cleft his brows. He looked dangerous.

She threw up her head, her chin tilting with something of his own arrogance. "Go right ahead, tell me. I'd like to hear just what you would do."

Strange lights flared in his eyes. His long, low, whispered "Damn!" came out with shivery harshness. "Why, damn you, Gena. You'd topple a saint's scruples!" His hands shot out explosively and closed over the fine bones of her shoulders. He pulled her back with him, eyes closed, on to the low swinging hammock.

But there was no need for force! Into Gena's life came that moment when she surrendered to the clamorous demands of her nature. His hands left her curving shoulders to cup her face, holding it motionless. There was no need. Gena turned her face up, blindly, her mouth parting like a thirsting flower. A tremor shot through her and a tumultuous quickening. He muttered something quite incoherent and took possession of her mouth so completely, so forcibly, that her whole body shuddered, then quieted against him. The world fell away from her and there was only the man and the night; the wind and the living stars.

He freed her soft mouth to find still softer skin, his two hands hard and caressing in the small of her back. She arched her body and a whisper fought its way up out of her subconscious.

"I love you ... I love you ... and I don't care about anything else!"

Tension flared in him, communicated itself instantly in the set of his head, his powerful shoulders, the stilled hands.

"The devil you do!" The words shot out low and violent. They brought her right out of the whirlpool of sensual excitement.

"Why ... why ..." She shrugged her long hair free from her face. "Let me up!"

His hand tightened, exerted just enough pressure to keep her still. "Stay right where you are. I prefer to retain the initiative. You just told me you loved me." His tone was so set and uncompromising that Gena found the courage to deny her own heart.

"Obviously I was lying," she said, her breath coming rapidly. "The effects of a short brandy. Why, I don't even *like* you!"

"I don't think you do either." He was watching her with his topaz eyes almost closed. "What happened now was just a case of a responsive young woman awakening to her own sensibilities."

"Oh, without a doubt." Her voice broke up a little, brittle, unhappy. "Don't give it another thought. I'm just a silly sentimentalist. But let me tell you, Mr. Brandt, I've been kissed one million times before tonight!"

His eyes sparkled menacingly. "That makes you an entirely different proposition!" He bent his dark head and she struggled wildly, but he fought her down, hands and mouth unbearably insistent. A minute passed and she went limp with that curious bonelessness that presaged surrender. Hot tears slid down from under her tightly closed eyelids and rolled on to her cheeks.

He tasted salt and lifted his head. "Damn, damn, damn!" he said half savagely, and brushed her hair off her fragile temples. "That's the whole trouble – you start out on brandy and end up on a crying jag!"

Gena rubbed a hand over her eyes. "I thought I was doing rather well for a woman who's been hotly desired and furiously scorned all in the one night!"

His voice was sardonic. "No man in his right mind would scorn *you*, Gena, I'd just like you to know what you're talking *about* before you say things like that to me."

She closed her eyes briefly, unable to look at him though he was etched into her brain.

"Well, you can set your mind at rest. I'll *never* say it again, believe me. I'll keep right out of your way."

"Just you try it!" His voice sounded inexpressibly grim and her eyes flew open. She stared at him in honest perplexity.

"I don't understand you. I don't understand you at all!"

He ran a finger down her short, straight nose.

"Is that to be expected? You're – what? Twenty-two, and a young twenty-two at that. I'll be thirty-six before I know it and I haven't exactly been fooling around all these years."

She broke away from him then, finding her feet and swaying unsteadily on them.

"I don't want to hear about your Boccaccian love life,"

she hissed at him vehemently, and put her hands over her ears. "I simply won't *listen*!"

He gave a great shout of laughter and came to his feet in one beautifully co-ordinated movement.

"I'll say this for you, Gena, no one can give me such a lift and a challenge!"

Beyond them through the trees headlights pointed fingers of light on the drive.

"It's the ute, isn't it?" He moved up beside her, his ear tuned to the sound of the engine. "The road must be open, the lights should be on soon. I think I'll wait and have a word with Frank." He put a hand on her shoulder. "Your *new* foreman, my dear. Go inside. There's no need for *you* to make an appearance."

"Oh no, I only *own* the show! Anyway, I shall pray for you," she said huskily. "Every moment. You're so wise, so terribly wise. *And* good!"

He turned on her a mocking grin and she felt a rush of pain and yearning. "Let's have a good long talk about it some time, shall we? Not now. Go inside."

"Why should I? I ask you! It's not often I get the opportunity for such friendly and constructive criticism."

"Yes, and it's a bit of a strain on our normal pattern. Now will you scat! Here are the Simmons. Have a nice hot cuppa with Thea if you must."

Gena obeyed without further demur. She walked into the house and out to her room. She brushed her hair, smoothed her throbbing mouth with cream, then lipstick. He might not have believed her, but love had come. It was her first love and she was very much afraid it would be her last!

163

CHAPTER XI

THE Pink Lagoon was a beautiful place, sheltered by feathery interlocking acacias, festooned by the waterlilies that gave it its name and alive with birds and butterflies. The cool green world was full of pale colour, delicate and lucent. So many greens! It would take a lifetime to capture those pale tints, Gena thought. The weeks had slid by in a haze of gold and Gena's days were filled with a deceptive tranquillity. She was sketching in earnest now and sending all her best efforts back to Delia Hunt, of *Koko, the Bush Koala* fame.

Most of the sketches captured the atmosphere of the bush; of beautiful places such as these. There were innumerable sketches of wild creatures, their calm dignity, their soft feet and eager eyes. Delia wasn't to know how many ephemeral adventures Gena had hopping tentatively through the undergrowth stalking a likely subject before it slipped away into shadow. There were sketches too of birds, all kinds of birds, from the tiny crimson chat to the powerful wedge-tailed eagle. In fact, Gena found so much subject matter on her doorstep that she was constantly working in a rage of delight.

On that hot, still morning she put her sketchbook down and turned to Becky sitting like a little queen, a coronet of yellow flowers in her hair.

"How are you, sweetheart? Having a lovely time?"

Becky nodded and looked up at her with her large clear

164

irises flecked with gold. She smiled and Gena felt her heart go out at the wistful quality of that smile. She took the childish hand, smoothing out the long frail fingers.

"One day, my little friend, you're going to sit beside me chattering like the birds up there. You're going to say 'Gena, teach me how to draw a goanna'. And it's going to be very soon. I just know it. Why, it might even be today!"

Becky rubbed her face against her like a kitten, caught in the spell of Gena's soft, hypnotic tone. She opened her mouth like a tiny bird, greatly daring – but no sound came out! Her small face was a mirror for her sadness and resignation.

Gena hugged her tight. "Now, now, don't worry so much about it, pet. Why, that naughty old voice has just slipped right down to your toes, but now it's on the way up. Why, very soon it's going to pop right out of your mouth when you least expect it. Look, I'll show you!"

Gena leaned over and picked up her sketchbook again, opening it at a fresh page. She began sketching little cartoon characters that looked like Becky chasing a runaway voice. They sat there for a few moments in that sun-dappled shade with the little girl resting against Gena's side, quietly entertained.

From the position of the sun it was getting on towards lunchtime and Keera would be waiting. Gena collected Becky's swimsuit and towel and shoved it into her bag along with her own things. She stood up, looking down at the child.

"We'd better go back soon, pet. Mummy will be waiting. Now I'm just going to have one more dip before we go back. It's so lovely! You sit here and wait for me. I don't want you to get wet again."

Becky nodded and Gena pulled off her yellow silk shift riotously printed with orange and pink flowers to reveal a brief matching bikini. She waded out into the water until she was waist deep, sweeping up her hair and securing it in a Grecian knot. Then she plunged into the stream and swam a little downstream with long clean strokes. It was heavenly! She turned and raced back through the cool green water like a slim golden arrow. Mid-stream she trod water, almost touching the sandy bottom. Becky waved to her and she waved back. She angled her way back to the back and stepped out on to a large flat rock.

"Pass me the towel, please, pet," she said idly, then stood stock still listening. Horses and riders were coming down the narrow bridle track. Becky too halted, looking upwards.

In a moment they swung into view – a familiar tall, lean figure and a young woman ... Barbara! For an instant Gena toyed with the idea of diving right back into the stream, but Becky was there too, waiting and watching intently, so she decided against it.

Both riders dismounted on the broad grassy stretch of higher ground, tethering their horses. Cyrus Brandt came swiftly down the steep embankment.

"What, not even a 'hello'!" he quipped lightly. Becky moved across to her uncle and pulled on his hand. He looked down smiling. "Now who might this little princess be? Introduce us!" He swept the child into his arms, kissing her sun-touched cheeks.

Barbara landed with a flurry of small stones. She looked

166

flushed and excited, her face curiously adult beneath the childish brown fall of hair.

"Hello there!" she said pleasantly. "You're keeping Mrs. Brandt waiting, you know. She wants to start lunch. I'm staying today." The very blue eyes travelled over Gena's brief swimsuit with unconcealed disapproval. "What have you been doing down here, anyway?"

"Sketching," Gena said in a crisp neutral tone. "I do a lot of it in a sympathetic atmosphere, but I don't think I'll be doing much more today!" She brushed past the cattle baron and heard his softly uttered "Miaow!"

Barbara took no further notice of her. She bent to Becky, commenting on her lovely wildflower coronet that Gena had made for her. Gena looked up in time to catch Cyrus Brandt's long, level stare. The look on his dark face, topaz eyes taunting, made her automatically angry.

"What are you trying to do, memorise me?" she asked bluntly.

He shrugged his powerful shoulders. "A thousand pardons, my lady, but I've already done that!"

Gena resisted the impulse to fling the towel at him.

"Hurry up now," he said, his eyes sparkling at her quick rise of hostility, "and we'll take you up to the house." He looked towards Barbara. "Could you take Becky up with *you*? I'll give Gena a ride. Baldar will take the extra weight."

Barbara looked her bewilderment. "Haven't you something *else* to put on?" she asked in a pointed, imperative tone, seemingly unable to continue looking at Gena's slim golden figure. Why, everything about the girl shone; eyes, skin, hair, dazzling in the white heat of the sun.

167

The cattle baron bent down and picked up Gena's yellow shift and passed it to her. She took it and pulled it furiously over her head, feeling long silky strands of hair coming away from the Grecian knot. Barbara took hold of Becky's hand and led her up the bank. There was no expression on *her* face at all!

"I'd much rather walk back," Gena was saying with a touch of heat.

His lean hand closed around her wrist tightly. "Then you won't know what you're missing!" He propelled her unresisting up the steep bank.

Baldar was waiting, fidgeting and pawing the ground; a magnificent temperamental animal, sixteen hands high, broad in the chest and withers, its satiny coat gleaming a reddish gold in the sun. The cattle baron put her up on its back, then mounted behind her, turning to see if Becky was quite happy. Becky was. She adored horses.

They covered the quarter mile in sparkling time. The wind whipped strands of Gena's long pale hair across his mouth and he blew them away again.

"You smell like a dryad," his chin hazed her ear, "all cool and green, and even your feet are bare, but you'll have to keep that hair out of my eyes."

Instinctively Gena put up her two hands to smooth the flyaway strands and his encircling arm tightened and bit hard into her. Baldar reefed and snorted, acting up. He quieted the big stallion with his hands on the reins, talking in a low crooning undertone. A flock of brilliantly coloured lorikeets burst into the air, circling the flying horses. It was a wonderful ride and Gena abandoned all thoughts of self-consciousness. She sank back against his hard

168

body, the deeply cleft chin clearing the top of her head. Just ahead of them Barbara, on her big bay gelding, was flying over the rising ground holding Becky with a firm confident hand. Even at that distance Gena could sense her disapproval of the arrangement.

They cantered through the big wrought iron gates, then slewed right to the stables. Bauhinia blossoms fell on to their heads and Gena brushed them away, tilting her head backwards a little to smile at him. Something about his expression evoked an uprush of warm blood that melted her bones. Some meaning registered, but she couldn't put a name to it. She kept her eyes on his dark face, still nearer now. Against the peacock sky his head, his clear golden eyes, the curve to his mouth, was clearly defined. There came over her such a rush of hot, sweet desire that she turned her head away with fierce urgency. He gave a low laugh and bent his head. The skin of her creamy exposed nape tingled. There was a moment of intense consciousness, a warm tide of feeling.

"Why did you do *that*?" she asked, her voice oddly jumpy. He was silent for a maddening moment, then his laughing breath fanned her cheek.

"I clean forgot you weren't Becky. Why, do you mind, my doe-eye innocent?"

Gena subsided against him, wordless.

Lunch was a light, delicious affair, but less enjoyable then usual. Barbara led the conversation with such an air of crisp assurance that boredom descended like a cloud. She made much of increased transport costs, seasonal fluctuations and the hundred and one problems attached to running a cattle station, while Gena ate sparingly, rather listless, barely listening; a reaction, she supposed, to the slackening of heightened sensibility. With no such excuse Keera continually looked downward, seemingly astonished by the number of nails she had on each hand.

The meal progressed, and Barbara, knowledgeable, wedded to mutual interests, held the cattle baron to this and that point of management. Gena, from under her lashes, derived a certain sour satisfaction from the fact he too was undeniably bored, though maintaining a casual and affable front. Keera, suddenly restless, turned to her brother-in-law. "Do you think we might have coffee out on the court?"

He gave her a slight smile, a depth of relief in his burnished eyes. "Not for me, my dear. I must go back to the yards for an hour or two. I want all the clean skins branded by this afternoon."

At once Barbara thrust back her chair with the decided impression that she had important things to attend to as soon as she was clear of the house. "Thank you so much, Mrs. Brandt," she said with an unruffled, unruffable air. "That was delightful!"

Keera inclined her head, a certain wry amusement pricking her boredom.

Barbara turned to the cattle baron, as straight and eager as an arrow. "Do you mind if I join you, Cy? There are a few points I'd like you to clear up for me. Things Brian and I were arguing about only this morning."

"Right, Barbara," the cattle baron said briefly. He glanced across to where Gena was holding a hand to her temple. "I'll run you back when you're ready to go."

Barbara followed him out of the house, already immersed in her problems, without a backward glance for the other two women.

"Heavens to Betsy, what an excessively boring young woman!" Keera murmured, a faint line between her brows.

"I've rather a bad head," Gena said quite truthfully. "If you don't mind, Keera, I think I'll get away."

Keera looked at her quickly. "I'll run you back, dear. Cy's just gone and we don't need to bother any of the men. You *have* lost a little of your bright colour. Too much sun, perhaps, and Barbara on top of it. I ask you! Now, have you got your things together,"

"Umm, all collected," Gena nodded.

"Good. I'll go and get Becky. She should have finished her lunch by now. Back in a moment." Keera walked out of the room, making for the sun porch where Mrs. Cassidy gave Becky a glass of milk and a sandwich.

While she was gone, Gena checked her straw bag: swimsuit, towel, shift, sunglasses, keys. Everything there. She stood up, tucking her ice blue shirt into her slacks.

Her head was thumping in earnest now . . . a kind of racing chaos of the mind. There was no logic at all to the sudden tightening of her stomach muscles. She must be sickening for something.

Keera staged quite a hunt for the keys to the station wagon, but in the end they had to take the jeep. Surprisingly for a woman who handled a horse superbly, Keera was a very bad driver, with no real feel for an engine. Keera put it another way as she crashed gears. "Shocking, aren't I? I'm no good at all without the automatic

171

transmission." Gena immediately offered to take over, but Keera only laughed and drove on undaunted. "We'll get there," she promised.

The jeep fairly hurtled along, coming much too fast into the bends. Once or twice Gena suggested a change down through the gears, but Keera only laughed, in no way perturbed. "I always forget about the clutch on these darn things," she explained over the agonised protest of the engine. They bounced over cattle grids and shot across the narrow wooden bridges that spanned the meandering creek.

Bauhinia's gates were cleared without incident, but Gena kept a firm hand on Becky to hold her back in the seat. At any moment, Gena felt the child could shoot forward and hit the windscreen. Keera drove on whistling through her teeth, seemingly oblivious to Gena's nervous tension. The jeep slashed along the dark green shadows and out into the brilliant sunshine again. The sun struck across the windscreen with an awful radiance, momentarily blinding them.

Gena felt the turn come up almost before she saw it. She braced her feet on the floor, her stomach heaving. Keera came into it much too fast. She jammed on the brakes and two wheels slipped off the hard surface of the road. The jeep went into a skid, with Keera vainly trying to turn the vehicle back on to the road.

Gena literally screamed at her, her heart in her throat.

"Don't, Keera! Don't try to straighten out . . . Go with the skid . . . Keera!" Her clear young voice echoed down the arches of the trees. Keera was panic-stricken, white to the lips.

The vehicle left the road and ploughed into the scrub with great paperbarks racing at them.

"Mummy!" The shrill, silvery word widened out into infinity. Keera's hand fell nerveless from the wheel. That agonised treble sent reverberations deep down into her soul. It clutched at her bursting heart and produced wild and hopeless panic. Gena leapt for the wheel, feeling an awful constriction in her throat. She crushed little moaning Becky up behind her, but there was no help for it. She grabbed the wheel with her two hands, holding it steady with all her might. Fear lent her superhuman strength and precision and with a wild sense of relief she felt the engine's resistance. It was all over in minutes.

The jeep safely negotiated the paperbarks only to nose at low speed into a felled tree trunk. Keera was flung forward over the wheel, blood trickling from her temple, her face ashen. Gena was flung backwards over the sobbing child. There was a moment of aching silence, then Becky's sobs broke out afresh . . . wet and noisy and . . . normal! Gena straightened up, pulling the child over on to her knees, cradling the frail little body. Keera was still bent over the wheel and Gena buried the child's face in her breast, reaching out to the mother, her hand almost nerveless with dread.

"Keera!" She was very nearly sobbing herself, holding the distraught child.

Keera's eyes opened, dazed and vacant, then they cleared with returning intelligence. "My God, so we're alive, then? I'll have to sit on your doorstep now for the rest of my life!" She turned to Gena, her eyes deep with gratitude, then she reached out for her child.

"Becky, my baby girl!" Her face was irradiated with love and tenderness; a true depth of feeling Becky was powerless to ignore. Nature reasserted itself and Becky went into her mother's arms saying over and over the single, indelible word: "Mummy! Mummy!"

Gena toppled out on to the grass feeling lightheaded with shock and relief. She sat down heavily in the shade of the trees watching the moving tableau. Keera seemed unaware of it, but her head was bleeding freely. Gena sat up suddenly and stripped off her shirt. She wore only a lacy white bra beneath it, but who cared! The sight of blood could have an adverse effect on an already over-wrought child. She moved back to the jeep, her legs, trembling, fashioning a rough bandage.

Ten minutes later Cyrus Brandt arrived at the spot. The big tyres of the station wagon sent up heralding spirals of dust. One of his outriders had spotted the jeep out of control, in the distance, and raced for the boss. He slammed out of the car racing towards them, his dark face taut with anxiety.

One look at Keera's transfigured face told him all he needed to know. His strong arms closed around mother and child. Gena moved back into the shadows. She had no claim on this family group. And that was how they appeared to her; an indivisible unit; man, woman and child. Her eyes filled with the tears of isolation more than self-pity. Cyrus Brandt put Keera and Becky tenderly into the front seat of the station wagon, then turned back, stripping off his own shirt. He walked towards Gena, his eyes never leaving her. He bent over and brought her to her feet, buttoning her wordlessly into his shirt, all-enveloping, warm from his body. Lean fingers brushed the tears from her cheeks, and his arm descended around her slight shoulders as he led her back to the car.

CHAPTER XII

FOR several days after that frightening experience Dr. Garrett compelled Becky to remain in bed. The child was to rest quietly. Those were his orders. No one on Bauhinia seemed able to grasp in its entirety the miracle that had happened to them – except Becky. She accepted the return of her voice with the lightning transition only children seem capable of. She sat up in her bed, protesting continually at her confinement, but her mother stayed with her reading stories; the whole series of Koko the Koala with Gena's charming illustrations; and for that week the two made friends all over again.

A week later Becky was allowed up, free to roam the property, and a great peace descended on Bauhinia; a peace that extended to the neighbouring Malaleuca. Summer was slipping imperceptibly into cooler weather and Gena took her morning's mail out on to the veranda to re-read it in the bright pool of sunshine. There was an enthusiastic letter from Delia commending her sketches and outlining her ideas for a new bushland series; a clinical, pre-natal dissertation from Linda and a warm, loving letter from her father, with news that Tony Carson was dating Raye Newell. Gena smiled and locked her hands behind her head. And Raye would very likely get him in the end! She lingered for another few minutes, seeing through the trees the men going out on a muster.

Frank Simmons was a first-rate cattleman and his policy was: 'a place for everything, and everything in its place!' For the past few days all the "scrubbers", the cattle that had gone bush, had been rounded up and brought in for dipping and branding. He was a wonderful improvement on Chad Duffy. As usual Gena's mind shied away from thinking about *that* man. He was just a horrible incident, best forgotten.

In another few days it would be Becky's fifth birthday and Keera was planning a family party. Bob Goddard was expected to fly in with Sir Joshua, Keera's father, and Gena was looking forward to meeting the old man. Her own gift was a portrait in oils of a tea-rose, based on the innumerable unnoticed sketches she had made of the child. The painting was progressing very well and Gena was pleased with it, especially as it would be such a surprise. She had the certain feeling that Keera would love it. She'd best get on with it!

A glint through the trees brought her to her feet. She stretched her arms above her head in a warm languorous movement, then moved over to the railing and leaned over it. It was Bauhinia's station wagon. She tucked her shirt in and tossed her loosened hair over her shoulder. It was the cattle baron. She decided to go down and meet him. Halfway across the dew-laden grass a fallen acacia branch suddenly came to life and slithered across her path.

Gena shrieked, her whole body recoiling in revulsion. The snake shot with incredible speed into the trees. Gena came on. She hurled herself at the man, who swung her, like a terrified child, clear of the ground.

"If you will fling yourself at me –" he murmured near

her ear, then lowered her gently to the ground. His hand stayed on her shoulder, neither advancing nor retreating.

Gena's breathing eased, steadied by his presence. "It's a snake!" she said tremulously.

"I know. It's harmless!"

She shuddered, her voice brittle with fright. "Oh, it's harmless. I'm sorry. I didn't know."

"Settle down now. You're always on about something or other. I'll get Frank to cut away a lot of the shrubbery."

She shot away from him as if she had been burnt, racing across to the safety of the veranda.

"Oh, go away, please. Leave me alone." She was oddly distraught.

He came after her, his voice a soft drawl. "I have a natural tendency to go away when told to do so. Do you really want me to?"

A fluid weakness went through her, a singular inability to answer. Bright tears caught in her eyelashes and trembled there. She could look no higher than the cleft in his chin.

He reached out and pulled her into his arms, tall and hard, full of a mocking indulgence.

"The time has come, my little spitfire, to make you an offer."

She blinked back her tears, her mind working furiously.

"You're after my property!"

"What else?"

"You don't deny it, then?" Her eyes flashed and her skin flushed a faint, furious pink.

He regarded her for a long moment, then propelled her

backwards into the house.

"It all depends. I mean . . . marriage. You're young, you're beautiful, you love me, you told me yourself, even if you don't *like* me, and I have a mind to take a wife . . . raise a family . . . maybe!"

For a moment Gena had the foolish notion that she would faint. Her face wore a look of utter stupefaction and she clutched at a chair.

"If this is a joke, it's in very poor taste!"

His laugh was slightly wry. "I've never been more serious in my life. Don't you think I can handle you?"

She stood stock still with her head in a rigid backward pose. "There's something I have to tell you that might change your mind."

"Fire away." The slow, rational drawl steadied her.

"I can't ever sell Melaleuca to *you*. Uncle Raff made that stipulation in the will. If I do I lose *everything*," she lied.

"Poor little girl!" he tut-tutted gently.

"You don't care?" Gena looked up at him, incredulous.

"Why should I? This is a big country, honey. The little bit you've got is all yours. Just let me develop it for you."

Gena was silent for a long time, then she said wearily: "I've heard of everything."

He looked at her, his eyes gleaming. "Well, there's nothing new under the sun. Besides, everyone has heard of a marriage of convenience. Much the best way too." His hand closed on the nape of her neck, and she strained away from him, more frightened by quick hot pleasure than anything else.

179

"Don't touch me. Don't you dare! If you think for one moment I would entertain such a cold-blooded proposition –"

His arms closed about her with sudden strength. The change of his mood seemed lightning.

"No mere chit of a girl is going to stand there and argue with me," he said with supreme arrogance, then laughed in her ear. "Marry me, Gena. You'll find it easier than you ever dreamed."

She hit out at him in a fury. "Who are you to think . . . to think . . . I'd want to be married to you!"

He held her tight against all her struggles. "Why, you stubborn, ungrateful, rebellious little wretch! There's only one sure way to quiet you." He hauled her into his arms, still fighting and panting. A hot rush of excitement slipped through her veins like a drug, then the surprised and shocked delight of his mouth on hers . . . dizzyingly new . . . disturbingly familiar. She would never be free of him now, never for a moment be free of his power over her. The moments of intolerable excitement shivered by. He pulled away first and looked down at her.

"There are plenty of good-looking women in the world, honey. I won't ask again."

A strange detachment stole over her. "I can't make you out."

"You can't make yourself out, you mean. The next step, my lady, is going to come from *you*. I'll take no more tongue-lashings!"

She looked at him nonplussed. "I may sell to the Langs," she said defensively.

He wasn't impressed. "Not the *Langs*, honey. You

won't get your price. Let Bob handle the sale for you if you *must* sell."

Her mouth parted. "You're just being clever!"

"Don't make excuses for me." He looked at her through half-closed lids.

She turned her head away from him, moody and withdrawn. "I suppose you realise you've created a sensation."

His mouth twitched. "Think about it, Gena. Is it *such* a surprise?"

She stared unseeingly back at him, trying to probe that mocking mask.

"There you go again! That exasperating ambiguity. You're getting at something. But what is it? I must know."

He didn't answer, his hands like a vice on her sweetly curving body.

Somewhere inside her a great wall broke. Wave after wave crashed over her head with a roar of silent ferocity. Her mouth clung to his with a completeness that blotted out all caution. Soon she would drown in this overwhelming wave.

"Cy!" she breathed in a kind of mad defiance, and locked her hands behind his crisp dark head.

Immediately he held her down to look into her eyes.

"Could it be you've changed your mind?" His burnished eyes were glinting with pure mockery and she broke away from him with surprising strength.

"Every little wild cat hates a cage!" he said, and smothered a laugh.

Her breath was coming raggedly. "Oh, but I hate you, Cyrus Brandt, and I'll *never, never, never,* change my mind!"

"And never is a long, long time. Chin up, honey. This too will pass!" Even the air was disturbed, heavy with the garden fragrance. Gena stood in the centre of the room staring across at him warily. His voice was very dry. "You look like you're on the point of imminent violence. As though it's inevitable between us. But it would be no contest at all. Now put a few things in a bag. Keera wants you to help her with some idea she's got worked out for the party."

Gena went quietly.

From that day on she knew no peace at all. She became a secret watcher and weigher of random words and looks, a sleepless arranger of this and that piece of evidence trying to arrange it into a pattern. All that emerged was ... *certainty*. Cyrus Brandt was the colour and shape of her existence. His very essence was carried around in her bloodstream. She was torn constantly between delight and panic – delight near to ecstasy in the warm memory of his lovemaking, panic at the thought of what it would inevitably mean.

Very soon now she would have to face up to her future!

CHAPTER XIII

THE town was idle, nearly deserted on that warm still afternoon. When Gena came out of the grocery store she was startled to see a man sitting, head down, on the bench against the railing that stood between the store and the lending library. She looked at the man again. There was something familiar about him. He lifted his head and turned his face to her, and her heart almost turned over with shock. It was Chad Duffy!

"Well, if it isn't Mr. Almighty Brandt's girl-friend!" he said with an odd, half sickly leer.

She gave a sharp, indrawn breath, and made an attempt to get past him. "Excuse me."

His eyes glittered with mockery. "No hurry, little lady. *I* waited for *you*. I've got a message for you. Pass it on to your boy-friend. Tell him he's got it comin' to him. I've got my own ways of getting even," he said with frightening vehemence.

Gena could only stare at the contorted face, the open pores that shone with sweat. "Get even ... for what?" she asked with a contemptuous kind of composure.

"For everything that's happened to me, that's what. I can't get a job *here* ... *anywhere* ... Not doing *nothin'*. He's cruelled me everywhere, in every way he knows how. Yes, he's a big man, Mr. Almighty Brandt!" He laughed a harsh, uncontrolled sound.

Gena spoke coldly, rationally. "I don't think he's given you a thought."

"Well, I've given him plenty. I've got all the time in the world. He's seen to that. There's only one thing I'm pleased about – I did him in with the old man. Cunningham swallowed everything I fed him . . . like a lamb! Got real senile there towards the finish."

Gena fought down a wave of nausea. She could see that this might have been so.

Duffy was watching her attentively, gloatingly, his eyes unnaturally bright. "Surprised you, didn't I, little lady?"

There was a sickening familiarity about the scene, as though it had happened before, preordained. She could only marvel at her composure.

"Let me past, Mr. Duffy," she said calmly. "It will do you no good to bring any further attention on yourself."

He thrust his face at her, alcohol heavy on his breath. "You see why, though, don't you? You see why I have to do it?" All at once in his green glowing eyes Gena could discern the catlike tongue of revenge . . . the silent menace of mental imbalance.

"You're surely mad," she said mechanically.

"Tell him before it's too late!" Duffy warned her.

Gena gazed back at him almost struck dumb. The words pounded into her brain. *Before it's too late*. They had a sinister significance beyond the man and the place. She forced herself to step closer to him, her hostility rising to match his own.

"Threats are dangerous to everyone, Duffy, including the one who makes them. *And* they're *punishable*! You'd do well to remember it."

Two women walked past them giving them covert, curi-

184

ous glances. Gena lifted her head, trying desperately to smile.

"Lovely day!" she said politely.

The women agreed and hurried on. Chad Duffy was not a man they would care to speak to!

"Yes, ma'am, it sure is a lovely day," Chad Duffy said strangely. "But there won't be too many more of them. Tell him!" The light struck glistening across the red-flecked whites of his eyes.

"You can be sure of that," she said in a tight, flat voice. "And he's a man who knows how to take care of himself." She turned and moved swiftly away from him with her head in a turmoil. She was unable to put Duffy and his threats out of her mind. Something about the man made her desperately panicky. The look in his eyes! Everything was so much more terrible than she thought. And she was responsible for it. She would have to tell Cy!

Later when she tried to speak to him about it he shrugged the whole subject away. Chad Duffy was the least of his worries; a confirmed no-hoper who had never done anything spectacular either way. Why, he hadn't even given the man a thought, much less spoken to anyone else about him. As Gena looked back at him, so tall and powerful, she thought she too had no reason at all for her fears. Yet they persisted! Strong and deep-rooted ... fears without name!

Ever afterwards Gena was to remember the afternoon of Becky's fifth birthday: the afternoon when her world almost came to an end. The day was so clear and still and hot that it might have been weather under glass. Everything in the garden took on an added, edged brilliance. They were all assembled on the lawn, Sir Joshua, a tall, spare, still handsome figure, Bob Goddard, Keera, Gena and Becky in a lemon voile birthday confection embroidered in blue. They were waiting for Cy before Keera took the colour shots for subsequent showing in the projection room. Cy was late and Keera was fussing. An hour's delay was an unusual occurrence for Cy. He had more than enough time to get back from Langlands where he had dropped off the vet.

Keera was looking flushed and lovely as she held tight to Bob Goddard's hand. Old Sir Joshua turned to Gena sitting so quietly at his side.

"I hope I'm being over-anxious, but I feel something's gone wrong; a sort of numbness in my old bones. I wouldn't say anything to Keera about it, but *you*, young lady, with your grave, serious eyes, tell me I'm worrying needlessly." He waved a rueful hand, looking at her for reassurance.

The first wave of panic struck! For a moment Gena was without words. Her face wore a haunted look.

"I can see we have a mutual worry," he said dryly, nibbling on his lower lip. "I thought so. Your tension was getting through to me, very clearly. Tell me about this man Duffy. Keera started out on the subject and then got sidetracked. I don't like the sound of it. Cy has always carried his fearlessness far beyond ordinary limits. It's been my experience, however, that the strongest man is at the disadvantage of an unstable opponent."

Gena's pale head was bent, her eyes wide and fixed. She

186

looked unseeingly into the scarlet ruffled heart of an hibiscus.

"Sir Joshua, you're frightening me!"

"I'm frightening myself, my dear," he said abruptly, and unlocked his fingers. "However did we get into such a conversation on such a beautiful afternoon with my little granddaughter restored to full health and happiness!"

"We're tuned to the same wavelength, I suppose," Gena said faintly, her stomach beginning to churn.

"You love him, don't you?"

"Is it so obvious?" She turned her head to look at him, a faint trace of pink in her cheeks.

"To old eyes like mine – yes, my dear. I admire Cy enormously. It was the wish of my life to have a son like him – or a son-in-law, for that matter. But he got away from us. Now all that is in the past. Keera's going to marry Bob Goddard, you know, after a reasonable time. I suppose she's told you?"

"Not as yet, Sir Joshua. She looks very happy. I don't think I've seen her looking so well and relaxed."

"Yes!" her father agreed slowly. "It's my most heartfelt desire that they should make a go of it. Keera gave Gavin a bad time of it. I shouldn't be saying that, I don't know why I did. It must have popped out unawares. Anyway, it's true. Bob, now, is an entirely different kettle of fish. If he can forget how much he's in love with her, it should work out. The gentle, diffident approach has never worked with Keera. Her nature demands a dominant mate." He looked across at his daughter with loving eyes. "Yes, she does look beautiful. She's mellowed a great deal. If only her mother was here today! She always used to tell me I was making a mistake with Keera, but I never would listen. I spoilt her dreadfully, you know. I must take the blame for a lot of Keera's mistakes."

Gena leaned over and patted his hand. "You didn't do too badly, Sir Joshua. Keera, I think, will make an outstanding woman. She's been through a great deal."

"Perhaps it's been the making of her," Sir Joshua observed quietly. "I'd like to think so."

Keera came across the lawn to join them, pressing an affectionate hand on her father's shoulder.

"Now what are you two nattering about so intently?" Her eyes crinkled with laughter. "If Cy's not here in another ten minutes I'm going to start without him – and *then* listen to the uproar! Becky, for one, won't smile." She broke off abruptly, looking her astonishment.

A rider was coming at full speed across the emerald green lawns – forbidden territory for horses. "Well, what the devil . . . !" Keera started out to say. Dave Wells, Bauhinia's foreman, was riding straight at them. Only feet away he slid off his sweat-lathered mare.

The herald of disaster! Gena thought, shuddering under the knowledge.

"There's been an accident – a terrible accident. The Boss!"

Gena heard no more. Her ears were filled with the wild roar of presentiment.

Dave Wells gagged on his breath and Bob Goddard raced forward to steady him. "For God's sake, man, what's up? You look on the point of collapse!"

The tableau had broken up. Old Sir Joshua started to his feet, his blue-veined hands shaking. Keera shouted

188

across the lawn for Mrs. Cassidy to come and take Becky into the house. Gena stood swaying on her feet. A great wave of desolation engulfed her, a flood of pain and grief. So this was to be the unalterable pattern of her life. Desolation! *Cy!* the name echoed crazily in her head, ringing, oppressive. There were white faces around her. "*Cy!*" She cried out his name as if she had been struck a fatal blow. Her young face was terrible to see. Sir Joshua lunged towards her, but too late!

Gena crumpled and pitched headlong to the ground.

When she opened her eyes again, she was lying on a couch in Keera's bedroom with Keera slapping her wrists and speaking her name.

"Gena, Gena dear."

Gena dragged herself back to an empty world.

"Oh, what a fright you gave us, you poor child! It wasn't what you thought. What any of us thought, including Dave. Cy is all right, my dear – just a flesh wound. If only we'd taken more notice of you! You warned us. Chad Duffy was waiting at the junction before the straight run in, with a rifle! Cy slowed for the turn and he fired, but thank God Cy had Bodalla with him. He gave the alarm and started barking. Duffy was stampeded into shooting precipitately. The bullet glanced off Cy's shoulder. He pulled off the road and Bodalla sprang at the man, dragging him backwards. I'm afraid he's in a bit of a mess, but more superficial than anything else. Cy called the dog off before any real damage was done."

"And Duffy, what's happened to him?" Gena asked, a little colour returning to her cheeks.

"Mick Ryan's taken him into custody. Doc Garrett's even stitched him up. Can you beat it? The devil looks after his own. Well, there you have it. Cy is quite all right. He's lost a little blood, that's all. It's *you* we're all worried about. I've never seen such a dead faint." Keera followed the direction of Gena's eyes. Becky was standing in the doorway, her black-lashed eyes enormous.

"Can I come in, please, Mummy? I want to see Gena." Her mother nodded her approval and Becky walked across the rust-coloured carpet. "Are you *very* sick, Gena?" she asked, her small face concerned.

"Sort of, sweetheart. But I'll be all right soon!"

"Well, don't be too long," Becky advised her very seriously, " 'cause Uncle Cy is going to hang my picture and he said we can't *pozz'bly* do it without Gena."

"I'm beginning to think we can't *pozz'bly* do without Gena, full stop." Keera leaned forward and kissed Gena's cheek. "Rest quietly for a few moments more. A brandy might help. Cy is getting it. Now come along, Becky my lamb, give Gena a kiss so she'll get better a whole lot quicker."

Becky obliged, pressing a sweet, moist kiss on the side of Gena's nose. "I love you, Gena, and I love my picture and so does everybody, and I'm sorry you're sick, but you've got to get up soon, 'cause Uncle Cy is going to hang my picture."

Gena smiled at the soft note of insistence. "All right then, that's a promise!"

After they had gone Gena shut her eyes again. She felt overwhelmingly tired, weary enough to close her eyes forever ... Was this the way one reacted to shock? A weary

190

body and a mind that found no outlet for its emotions. She sank further down on to the couch and turned her face into the silken comfort of cushions.

How long he'd been standing there she didn't know. She only knew her body reacted with a mind of its own! She flung herself to him without a word or a cry, locking her arms around him, hugging him to her, with a furious need and abandon, an abandon that was tempered with sadness. She could hear the rhythmic beat of his heart beneath her cheek. Or was it her own heart? Or two hearts that beat in deepest empathy? She burrowed her face into him in an aching need for contact.

His hand on her hair lifted her face to him.

"Well?" his eyes demanded her complete surrender.

She shook her head slightly from side to side, even at that moment unsure of him.

"If you'd only explained to me, Cy. Even three good reasons would have done!"

His beautiful, burnished eyes still retained a glimmer of mockery.

"My stubborn little love, you won't bow down to me, will you! But if you really need reasons, I can give them to you." His strong, lean hands cupped her head. Her eyes were very clear and steady under their tilting brows.

He bent his dark head and gave her a hard, swift kiss. "First – I love you. Second – I love you," he kissed her more completely now. "And third . . ."

". . . I love *you*." She stood on tip-toe and stopped his mouth with her own. He didn't seem to mind that her voice was half incoherent.

When later Gena was able to lift her head her mouth was crimson and her eyes were wide and brilliant.

"But what shall I do with Melaleuca?" she asked him, a little breathless.

He lifted her off her feet and carried her back to the silken pile of cushions.

"Keep it for our son!"